S0-AXB-640

Burying the Hatchet

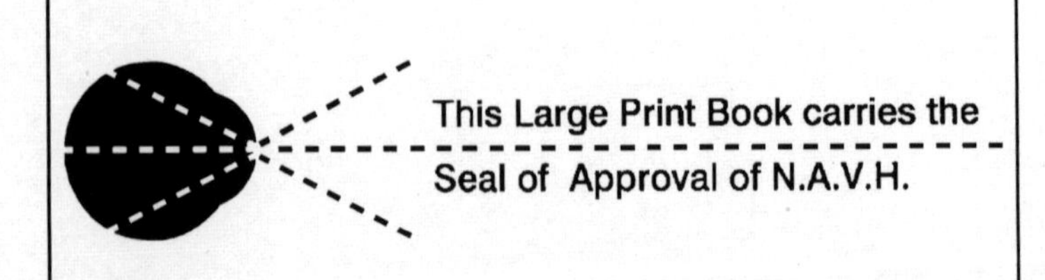
This Large Print Book carries the
Seal of Approval of N.A.V.H.

A KENTUCKY GEEZERS MYSTERY,
BOOK 2

Burying the Hatchet

Chris Well

THORNDIKE PRESS
A part of Gale, Cengage Learning

Detroit • New York • San Francisco • New Haven, Conn • Waterville, Maine • London

All scripture quotations are taken from the King James Version of the Bible.
Thorndike Press, a part of Gale, Cengage Learning.

Thorndike Press® Large Print Christian Mystery.
The text of this Large Print edition is unabridged.
Other aspects of the book may vary from the original edition.
Set in 16 pt. Plantin.

LIBRARY OF CONGRESS CATALOGING-IN-PUBLICATION DATA

Well, Chris, 1966–
Burying the hatchet / by Chris Well. — Large print ed.
p. cm. — (Thorndike Press large print Christian mystery) (A Kentucky geezers mystery ; no. 2)
Originally published: Uhrichsville, Ohio : Barbour Pub., c2011.
ISBN-13: 978-1-4104-3755-6
ISBN-10: 1-4104-3755-8
1. Retirees—Fiction. 2. Murder—Investigation—Fiction. 3. Kentucky—Fiction. I. Title.
PS3623.E4657B87 2011
813'.6—dc22 2011005517

Published in 2011 by arrangement with Barbour Publishing, Inc.

Printed in Mexico
1 2 3 4 5 6 7 15 14 13 12 11

This one is dedicated to my aunt Jean.
Thank you for believing in me!

CAST OF CHARACTERS

Earl Walker does not want to believe his new pastor would commit murder — but the proof is overwhelming. Now, if he could just figure out how to break it to Gloria . . .

When **Gloria Logan** first met Earl, she had to convince him she was innocent of murder. Now can she convince him she's guilty of loving him?

Jenny Hutton pressured Earl into solving a full-fledged murder mystery that time at Candlewick Retirement Center. Now that the pastor is in trouble, can she get him to do it again?

Deputy Landon Fisher is just trying to do his job. But Jenny and these two pesky senior citizens keep trying to do it for him. . . .

THE VICTIM AND THE SUSPECTS . . .

Montague Black was a celebrity psychic riding his way to national fame by intruding on a local murder investigation. What was the secret to Montague Black's amazing powers?

Pastor Andrew Benton, minister at New Love Fellowship, waged a public war with the so-called psychic. Did he commit murder in the name of the Lord?

Divina Zuniga nabbed the celebrity psychic with a national television deal. When he got a better offer, did she kill to seal the deal?

Jack Carpenter was the business manager for the victim. Did he cancel his client's contract permanently?

Hamilton Page was writing a book on the "Mercy Killer" murders. When the psychic refused to participate, did the author close the book on him?

Sheree Jackson, activities director at Heritage Care, claimed to be a former lover of the victim. Was she a woman scorned?

Prologue

Deputy Landon Fisher was driving Sheriff Meyer to the scene, when the older man told him to stop off for coffee. Landon blinked. "Shouldn't we step on it, Sheriff?"

"No need to get in a panic, Landy. Doc Semple is on the scene. Besides, the body ain't gonna just get up and walk away before we get a chance to talk to it."

The waitress returned with two steaming cardboard cups with plastic lids. Landon sipped on his coffee, barely noticing the burned flavor.

The call had come in that morning, a death overnight at Heritage Care. Normally, it would not be unusual for someone to pass away there; the residents were primarily the aged and failing, all just waiting for the end.

No, what made this a cause for concern was that in the past few weeks there'd been a couple of murders — and both victims were senior citizens. If this also turned out to be a murder, it could mean that Fletcher County, Kentucky, was home to its very own serial killer.

The drive up Old Miller's Road was uneventful. The deputy, behind the wheel, watched the scenery go by — trees, grass, and rocks, broken up by the occasional farm. The cruiser took the frequent hills and turns fair enough, though the aging shock absorbers clearly needed attention.

They drove past a rusty old tractor at the side of the road. It looked like some museum piece, but they knew that Charlie McGrath only left it there the week before when it broke down. It took time to find replacement parts for the old tractor.

Landon grumbled to himself. "You'd think someone would have some pride."

"Now, stop that fidgetin'," Sheriff Meyer said. "We don't know that we'll even find anything suspicious."

"But what if we do? Have you thought about the ramifications if this is another murder?"

"Whoo-ee! The words they teach you in school."

"I just meant —"

"I know what you meant, son. And if you're right, I'm sure all manner of government folk will be more'n willin' to grab the reins. But let's not get that wagon out quite yet — the horse still ain't left the barn."

"And then if Montague Black gets involved again —"

"Trust me," the sheriff said, his voice lowering to an uncharacteristic growl, "if'n that psychic feller shows up again, I'm not about to let some showbiz type tell me how to do my job."

The deputy drove on a bit. Finally he got up the nerve to ask, "But what if he's actually channeling some kind of psychic energy? Don't you worry that —"

"That man's just a con artist."

"But if he can —"

"I'm done talkin' about him."

At the intersection by the Russell farm, they were stopped by a tractor, a wagon, and a lot of straw in the middle of the road. The deputy shifted into PARK. "What now?"

Obie Withers, a wrinkled old man with one crippled arm, struggled with his straw. Some of the bales had broken open.

The sheriff greeted him. "How's it goin' there, Obie? Havin' trouble haulin' again?"

Obie looked up from the pile. He offered a toothless grin. "Ayup, Sheriff."

Landon shouted in his most officious tone, "We've got to get this out of the road!

The sheriff and I are headed to a crime scene!"

"Hush now!" The sheriff flashed a warning glance at the deputy then grinned at Obie. "Can we help you get loaded back up?"

"I be mush oblished." The old man must have left his dentures at home.

The sheriff and deputy each grabbed a couple bales and threw them on the wagon. It quickly became apparent that the wagon needed to be completely restacked, or it would just spill onto the road again at the next stop.

When they had finished, Landon jumped back into the patrol car. He tried to ignore the scratches forming on his hands and forearms — not to mention the thick, sweet smell of hay now embedded in his uniform. He just wanted to get on his way. Once the sheriff was back in the car, he hit the gas. "We shouldn't have taken the time to reload his wagon."

"Now, if we'd just left Obie to fend for hisself, there coulda been some kinda accident. S'pose someone came 'round that curve and wasn't lookin' —"

"I just hate getting to the crime scene so late."

"You gotta relax, son. Maybe it'd help to

get your mind off things. If we weren't drivin' out here, what would you be doin'?"

"Right now? I guess filing paperwork."

"A day like today? The sun's out, son. Have a little imagination. This'd be a great day for doing some patrollin', don'tcha think?"

"I guess." The deputy grinned out his window at the passing trees. "I guess I could check how things are going down by the fishing hole. There's this great spot down behind my grandma's house."

"Think so?" Sheriff Meyer squinted. "You think there might be a lot of crime taking place down there?"

"But you said —"

"I said you could do your shift outside. Didn't say you could play hooky."

"Oh. I'm sorry. I didn't understand what you were asking."

"Don't worry about it, son." They drove on. "Now, if you were talkin' 'bout that creek down by the Watkins farm — now that's a place to set up a command post."

Landon looked at the sheriff. "Yeah?"

"Providin', o' course, you kept within earshot o' your radio."

The deputy turned onto the gravel drive for Heritage Care and parked close to the front. As they went inside, Sheriff Meyer pulled off his hat.

Eyes adjusting to the indoor lighting, Deputy Fisher took note of the worn turquoise carpeting, the chipped paint on the walls, the grime on the glass door behind him. He turned to the sheriff. "Where do we go now?"

The older man tapped him on the elbow and pointed to a little card taped to the wall: OFFICE. Wiping one hand on his official brown pants, Sheriff Meyer followed the direction of the arrow, down the hall.

The deputy followed. "What if it's another murder?"

Meyer let out an exasperated sigh. "Why don't we put less energy into all this frettin' and more into seein' what the doc has to say?"

Landon bit his lip as they passed a series of unlabeled doors. A bulletin board held a variety of bright-colored slips of paper, each bearing a printed announcement.

They reached the office. The woman behind the desk gave them directions to the victim's — that is, the deceased's — quarters, room 363. The doctor was already there, along with the manager of the facility, she told them.

Sheriff Meyer thanked her for the information and flashed a smile. It was that smile that always got him reelected. Even as his temples grayed, it only made him more distinguished. He reminded Fisher a little of Sean Connery, although the deputy would never admit that to the sheriff.

In room 363, they found Doc Zacharias Semple standing over the body on the bed. Nearby, a man in an ill-fitting navy suit wrung his hands. He looked about fifty, balding, with a hooked nose like a bird's beak.

The deceased was an elderly woman, her wrinkled face completely at peace. No visible wounds or signs of trauma — at least, not from where the deputy stood.

The man watching reached for a handkerchief and wiped his forehead. When he noticed the two lawmen, he stepped toward them. "This is awful — simply awful!"

"Hello, sir. I'm Sheriff Neil Meyer, and this is Deputy Landon Fisher. We're sorry for your loss."

"I'm just thinking what this means for our facility. Ever since the state shut down Candlewick, they've been watching the rest of us like a hawk. And now to think there's been a murder!"

"Well," the sheriff drawled, "we won't know that until the doctor gives a verdict. Let's hope for the best."

The doctor let out a sigh. "Until we get the body back to the table, I can't say for sure. But the preliminary examination doesn't really tell us anything." He snapped the rubber glove on one hand. "The deceased has been dead a good six or eight hours, give or take. Could very well have died in her sleep. If it weren't for the circumstances, it would be easy enough to assume natural causes."

The sheriff scratched his head. "That your verdict, huh?"

"That's all I can say right now. I was waiting for Jimmy to get here with his camera."

Jimmy Talbot was the photographer for the *Mt. Hermit Gazette-Torch.* He also doubled as crime scene photographer on the rare occasions that called for it.

Sheriff Meyer nodded. "When's Jimmy gonna get here?"

"He was taking pictures at the school soccer match. He didn't expect he'd be much longer."

Landon watched the sheriff examine the surroundings. The sparse, square room was lined by grungy tile on the floor, there was chipped green paint on the walls, and worn brown-striped curtains were pulled across the windows. The bulky air-conditioning unit under the window offered hot or cold air, depending on how you rotated the knob.

Nothing looked out of place. There was no evidence of a struggle. But then, the previous two murder scenes were found in more or less the same condition. The deaths had been ruled natural causes. In fact, if it had not been for the timely help of —

"Montague Black!" The sheriff's voice only sounded pleasant.

Landon turned to see the celebrity psychic standing in the doorway, big as life. The man's entourage crowded behind him, a cameraman taking in the scene. "It is good to see you again, Sheriff Meyer. I knew you'd come."

The sheriff held up his hat to fend off the camera. "Now, this here's a crime scene. I'm afraid none of you folks are authorized —"

"But we've already been here, Sheriff."

Sheriff Meyer turned a disbelieving stare on Doc.

The other man simply shrugged. "Who do you think called and reported that this woman had died?"

CHAPTER ONE

Sunday morning at New Love Fellowship, Earl Walker wheeled himself out of the new-members' class. His lady friend, Gloria Logan, waited for him in the hall. As they headed to the sanctuary for the service, she grabbed onto the back of his wheelchair and pushed.

Amid the noise in the hall, Gloria leaned over and spoke into Earl's ear. "So, what'd you think?"

"It was fine." Earl rubbed a hand over his closely cropped white hair. He watched the bustle as she navigated his wheelchair down the hall.

Earl still felt like a newcomer at church, even though he had been attending as Gloria's guest for a few months now. Prior to that, he had not been inside any church since the death of his wife, Barbara.

In the foyer, Earl and Gloria met up with their young friend, Jenny Hutton. A pretty girl in her twenties with long blond hair, she wore a dark blouse and skirt. She was adjusting her glasses when she saw them. "Mr. Walker! How was class?"

"Fine," Earl grunted. As they made their way through the hall, they were greeted by various members. Earl was still uncomfortable meeting new people. With the encouragement of Gloria and Jenny, he was becoming a little more acclimated outside his comfortable shell. But there were still limits.

Gloria waved to a friend across the foyer. "Do you mind if I go tell Bea something?"

"We'll meet you inside." Earl put his hands to the rims of his wheels and maneuvered toward the sanctuary.

Jenny leaned close. "So, how are things going?"

"Fine."

"I meant with you and Gloria."

"I know what you meant."

"And . . . ?"

"Nothing to report." Earl tried to ignore the feelings now stirring, the frustration of not knowing how things stood with Gloria. The frustration that he didn't know how to ask.

Instead, he focused on wheeling himself through the double doors into the main sanctuary. He navigated in and out of foot traffic, parking his wheelchair by the last pew.

Jenny grabbed three copies of the Sunday morning bulletin and handed one to Earl. She scooted into the pew, leaving space for Gloria on the end next to Earl.

Earl saw Pastor Andrew Benton making his rounds before the service. He was still amazed that the pastor and his family took him in when he lost his home at Candlewick Retirement Center. Prior to that, Earl had not been in church for more years than he cared to admit — and was touched to see that the folks at New Love Fellowship Church would reach out to him, a stranger, with such compassion.

The man flashed his pearly whites and put a hand on Earl's shoulder. "How's your new-members' class going? Is Gloria getting you through it all right?"

"It's . . . enlightening. The teacher is helping me learn how to find the things in the Bible we can know — and to trust God for those things we can't."

"Good to hear." Pastor Benton leaned over and shook Jenny's hand. "Hello, Jenny. Keeping up with your college studies?"

"You know it, Pastor."

"Great! I'll talk to you folks later." He flashed them one last smile and moved on to the congregants across the aisle.

Earl turned to Jenny. "I like him."

Her eyes widened.

"What?" he asked.

"I've never heard you say that about anybody."

"All part of my growth as a person." He saw Gloria across the sanctuary. He waved, even though it was unnecessary — they always sat in the same place. Both women preferred it closer to the front, but they accommodated him.

Gloria got to her seat. "Did you miss me?"

"I always do."

As the time ticked closer to the start of the service, more and more folks found their places. While Gloria and Jenny chatted with those in the next pew, Earl checked his copy of the bulletin. He always liked to prepare for the service. It gave him a sense of order. In all his years as a metro bus driver, that was the part of the job he appreciated most: Everything was worked out in advance.

The first hymn listed was number 467, "Trust And Obey." Earl tore off a small corner of his bulletin and bookmarked the hymnal. He did the same with the second hymn, number 598, "O Word of God Incarnate."

The scripture reading listed was Matthew

4:4. Earl took his Bible — which Gloria had given him — and marked the passage.

Consulting the bulletin again, he saw that this morning's sermon was going to be "Spiritual Hunger and God's Word," the third part in the series "*Foundations of Our Faith: Why We Believe.*" Earl clicked open his ballpoint pen and made a notation in his notebook. He wrote down the day and date, the sermon title, the series title, and Pastor Benton's name.

The pianist signaled the start of the service as an older gentleman shuffled to the pulpit. "Good morning, brothers and sisters," his voice crackled. "We want to welcome each and every one of you to the house of the Lord this morning." He asked the members of the congregation to bow their heads, and he prayed over the service.

Next at the pulpit was the music minister, Pete Donaldson. Earl, hymnal turned to the correct page, allowed himself a grin.

The music minister announced, "I know what hymn is listed in our bulletins, but we're going to sing something else this morning. Let's all turn to number 513 in our hymnals, 'Soldiers of Christ, Arise.' "

Earl's grin disappeared. As the congregation stood and followed the minister's lead, Earl fumbled with the pages. He didn't find it until they were halfway through the second verse.

After the hymn, one of the deacons took the pulpit. He announced the scripture reading which, to Earl's consternation, turned out to be different, too. Now it came from Acts chapter 8, verses 9–11 and 18–23:

> But there was a certain man, called Simon, which beforetime in the same city used sorcery, and bewitched the people of Samaria, giving out that himself was some great one:
>
> To whom they all gave heed, from the least to the greatest, saying, This man is the great power of God.
>
> And to him they had regard, because that of long time he had bewitched them with sorceries. . . .
>
> And when Simon saw that through laying on of the apostles' hands the Holy Ghost was given, he offered them money,
>
> Saying, Give me also this power, that on whomsoever I lay hands, he may receive the Holy Ghost.
>
> But Peter said unto him, Thy money perish with thee, because thou hast thought that the gift of God may be purchased with money.

Thou hast neither part nor lot in this matter: for thy heart is not right in the sight of God.

Repent therefore of this thy wickedness, and pray God, if perhaps the thought of thine heart may be forgiven thee.

For I perceive that thou art in the gall of bitterness, and in the bond of iniquity.

Earl barely found the passage in question before the reading was finished. What's the point of printing an order of service if you're not going to follow it?

The deacon went on to the morning's announcements: The soccer moms were having a bake sale; the children's church was taking some sort of field trip; the women's Bible study group was going to be discussing the book of James. Given how things were going, Earl had his doubts.

"And finally," the man said in a soft voice, "many of you have no doubt heard about the murder yesterday."

Earl's ears perked up. He'd just skimmed the paper that morning and hadn't read anything about a murder.

"We just want to pray this morning for the woman's family," the deacon said. "And for the police to find this awful killer before he strikes again."

Earl frowned. Strikes again? He really needed to get home and read his paper.

After the announcements, the music minister returned to the pulpit to lead the congregation in another hymn. Earl didn't even try to look it up.

His thoughts kept circling around the news of the woman's death. Who was she? Another senior citizen dropped off at the home and forgotten? Or had she been blessed with a family who still cared?

Earl thought back to another murder, months earlier. At Candlewick Retirement Center, a man named George Kent had collapsed at a party and died during the night. Everyone assumed it was just another case of a man dying of old age.

Only Earl had suspected foul play. By the time the ordeal was over and the killer was caught, Earl had annoyed a lot of folks around Candlewick, at least one false arrest was made, and the place shut down. It was quite a couple of weeks.

The hymn ended, and Pastor Benton took the pulpit. Earl grasped on to some small hope that at least the pastor would not deviate from his own order of service.

That hope didn't last long. "As you may have noticed, we haven't been following our original plan for this morning's service," the pastor began. "That's because events in the news have demanded a swift response — so I'm not speaking on the topic listed in the bulletin."

Earl clicked his ballpoint pen and scribbled out his careful outline.

"As mentioned earlier, there was another senseless murder this weekend. And, of course, that's a horrible thing. We just pray that the mighty Lord will swoop down with His sword of justice and split the truth from the lie and assist the police with a speedy conclusion to the investigation."

He paused. There was something unusually statesmanlike about his manner, like he was getting on a soapbox. Not at all the friendly demeanor with which Earl was familiar.

Pastor Benton continued. "But there is another facet to this circumstance that we should not take lightly — the intrusion of the forces of darkness. My friends, there is an occult figure who has inserted himself into the investigation."

Earl leaned over and whispered to Gloria, "What is he talking about?" She didn't reply. He really did need to get back to his newspaper and figure out what was going on.

The pastor pounded his fist on the podium. "I am, of course, talking about this so-called 'psychic detective' who has offered his services to the police in this matter."

Earl wrinkled his brow. Some psychic? The pastor was all bent out of shape over that?

"Let us turn now in our Bibles to Exodus 22:18. It says, 'Thou shalt not suffer a witch to live.' " Pastor Benton looked up from his Bible. "It sounds pretty plain, doesn't it? Now let's turn a few pages over to Deuteronomy 18:10. 'There shall not be found among you any one that maketh his son or his daughter to pass through the fire, or that useth divination, or an observer of times, or an enchanter, or a witch.' That's pretty black and white, too, isn't it? And yet, our society has become too cavalier about supernatural matters. People think that the things of the supernatural are just toys to play with, just harmless diversions."

Gloria murmured in Earl's ear, "If the pastor gets this worked up just seeing the man's name in the newspaper, can you imagine the fireworks if the two of them were put together in the same room?"

Earl nodded. He really needed to get home to his newspaper.

After church came the navigating again. Gloria and Jenny dillydallied just long enough with their purses and their bulletins, exchanging pleasantries with other folks, that they got caught in line. Earl was impatient, but his mind was still on the sermon. Not so much the stuff about the psychic, but the news that a murder had been committed, and that the victim was a senior citizen in a nursing care facility. It struck Earl way too close to home.

In the line, a woman remarked to Gloria, "Don't you think it's just awful? Pastor Benton getting all tangled up over the situation. It's not seemly."

Gloria asked, "How do you mean?"

"Whether or not the police need help with their little murder case —"

Earl snorted to himself. *"Little" murder case?*

"— has nothing to do with the matters of the church. The things of God and the things of man are separate. 'Never the twain shall meet.' That's what the Bible says."

Gloria frowned. "The Bible says no such thing."

"Well, I don't know exactly where it says that, but I know it does."

"Now, Maybelline, until you look it up in your own Bible and can point to it with your own finger, you better stop telling folks what is and is not in the Bible. Otherwise you're bearing false witness." Gloria paused. "Now, you do know where it says that, right?"

Earl glanced at the woman, who was now fuming. "I didn't ask to be preached at."

The two women separated as the crowd dispersed into the parking lot. Gloria leaned toward Earl's ear. "I don't think I quite handled that right."

"You sounded fine to me."

"I shouldn't have provoked her. You know, 'A soft answer turneth away wrath.' "

"Uh-huh." They were almost to the car. "Who said that?"

"It's in Proverbs. I'll show you sometime."

"That's important to you, isn't it? Not just quoting the Bible, but knowing where the passage is."

"It's the only responsible way to do it. Too many folks like to throw a bunch of religious words around to sound important. But if it's not genuinely anchored in the Bible —" She stopped at the car, searching her purse for the keys.

Earl asked, "And . . ."

She looked up from her purse and smiled. "I'm sorry. I was starting to preach there, wasn't I?" She opened the passenger door and helped him out of the wheelchair and into the seat. Then she took his wheelchair behind the car, folded it, and deposited it in the trunk.

When she got to the driver's seat, Gloria pulled her sunglasses off the visor. She put the keys in the ignition.

Earl said, "I don't mind."

She looked at him and grinned. "Don't mind what?"

"When you preach."

She blushed. "Well . . ."

He started feeling kind of warm himself. "So, what do you want to do for lunch? How about that fish place, Skipper Dan's?" It wasn't fancy, but the fish was crisp and easy for Earl to eat with his dentures. And he liked the hush puppies. It was also well lit.

"Actually," Gloria said, "I thought maybe we could have lunch at my house."

Earl felt his head bobbing slowly. He saw Jenny passing by and rolled down his window. "Hey, College! Wanna come to lunch?" He could almost hear Gloria grumble to herself. But she was too polite to make a fuss. And he was too nervous to be alone with her.

Jenny came to the window. "I don't want to intrude."

"No, we'd love it. Besides, we can discuss today's sermon." He turned to Gloria. "You don't mind, do you?"

Gloria's smile looked a little forced. "Of course not." She leaned toward Earl's window and yelled, "The more the merrier!"

When they arrived at the complex where Gloria lived, she helped Earl out of the car and back into his wheelchair. Inside, the ladies deposited him in the living room in front of the small television. Earl fumbled with the remote while they went into the kitchen to prepare lunch.

Gloria's TV didn't have many channels — just what the rabbit ears and the digital converter box could get. Earl flipped from channel to channel in a futile attempt to find something to distract himself. There was a local travel show. Some book discussion. A golf tournament. A documentary about a talking bird. A program about Jane Austen.

Earl turned toward the kitchen and shouted, "Hey, got today's newspaper?"

Gloria came out, wiping her hands on a towel. "I don't get the Sunday paper."

"Oh." He hid his disappointment badly.

"I'm sorry."

"Don't worry about it." As she went back to the kitchen, he turned again to the TV. He heard her resume the conversation with Jenny. He couldn't quite make out what they were saying over the sound of frying.

He flipped through some more channels: an infomercial about some new kitchen gadget, Boris Karloff dressed up as an Oriental man, men sitting in a boat waiting for fish.

Earl flipped to the next channel and there it was–a report on the so-called psychic that had Pastor Benton all a-fluster. The screen showed a tall, slim, dark-haired man holding court outside under the awning of some public facility, a shorter, rounder, blond man with spectacles at his side. They seemed to be holding something of a press conference. The red bar across the bottom of the screen announced in bold white letters, DETECTIVE FROM BEYOND? MONTAGUE BLACK, CHANNELIST.

The voice-over was saying, ". . . since the first murder was reported. The case has now become a matter of national attention."

The so-called psychic said in a flat, controlled voice, "Spiritual waves are a matter of scientific certainty. You merely have to be able to read them, not unlike radio waves traveling through the air — you cannot see them, but trained personnel can discern their meaning."

Earl barely noticed the aroma coming from the kitchen. The picture changed to a wide shot of the police investigating the grounds of a facility. They worked behind the protection of yellow tape and barricades.

The voice-over said, "And, in fact, the police wouldn't have even been aware that a crime — or crimes — had been committed, had it not been for the help of Montague Black."

"What's that you're watching?" Gloria reentered the room, bringing Earl a cup of hot tea. He didn't answer, his eyes intent on the television.

"Sources say that without the unorthodox testimony of the celebrated channelist, there would have been no reason to consider the three murders connected. However, the sheriff maintains he does not need the help."

The screen cut to a uniformed man, his salt-and-pepper hair matted as if he'd just removed his hat. The red bar at the bottom of the screen pegged him as SHERIFF NEIL MEYER. He was saying, ". . . no evidence at this time to support the use of any so-called psychic forces. We continue to trust the tried-and-true methods that've solved crimes around here for a hunnerd years."

Earl had to wonder whether this was the same guy who ruled the original murders as "natural causes." The reporters nipping at the sheriff's heels seemed to wonder the same thing, but he ignored them as he stepped back behind the protective barricade. He conferred with his deputies, one of whom Earl recognized as Landon Fisher.

The screen cut back to the news studio, where the plastic newscaster began to report on a hat festival. Earl grabbed the remote and muted the TV, glancing over at the dining area. Jenny placed three sets of silverware on the dining room table.

Gloria set out the food. It looked liked chicken-fried steak, mashed potatoes, and some green vegetable on the side. She looked at Earl. "Now can you tell us what that was all about?"

Earl grunted, wheeling himself to the table. "The recent murders. Apparently, this prophet guy is helping the sheriff."

Gloria looked at him. "Sheriff Meyer? And I suppose Deputy Fisher, too?" She clucked her tongue against her teeth. "They need all the help they can get."

Everyone seated around the table, they clutched hands to pray. Earl was still tentative about praying out loud, but the ladies insisted.

As they dug in, Jenny said, "I think Landy is cute." She curled some strands of blond hair behind her ear. "I mean, Deputy Fisher."

Earl, fork and knife in hand, got to work on his chicken-fried steak. He glanced in Gloria's direction. "Now when they arrested you that time, it was a simple mistake." He saw Gloria's face and realized he'd started down a bad road. He turned his eyes back to his meat. "Now, what about this psychic business? You know, this prophet guy helping the police solve these crimes?"

Jenny wiped her mouth. "You're confusing your terms. A prophet gets his information from God. A psychic gets his information from demons."

Earl scowled at her. "Are you serious? You're telling me a man with uncanny insight is actually some kind of demon priest?"

"I don't remember saying any of those words. I'm just saying — that is, the Bible says — if a person gets his power from the supernatural, there are only two sources available. Either he gets it from God, or he gets it from demons. There is no third option."

Earl challenged her. "And that's in the Bible?"

Jenny nodded. "Uh-huh."

Gloria stabbed a few peas. "Did they say anything about the victims?"

Earl got back to cutting his meat. "They

said that the three deaths were connected, and that this prophet — um, this psychic guy — seems to be really helping."

"Hey!" Jenny grabbed the remote off the coffee table and pointed it at the TV, turning on the sound. A photo of their church was onscreen, a banner across the bottom proclaiming, VOICE OF ANDREW BENTON, PASTOR OF NEW LOVE FELLOWSHIP CHURCH.

The voice out of the speaker was tinny but certainly the pastor's: "When the devil prowls about, he's not wearing his true appearance. The Bible says he appears as an angel of light. And now this so-called angel is down at the sheriff's office, trampling on a murder investigation!"

Gloria covered her mouth with her hand. "That's from this morning's sermon."

The picture cut back to the newscaster. "Benton's voice was recorded by a parishioner on his cell phone. Meanwhile, celebrated psychic Montague Black continues to capture the attention of the nation. And he's signing a deal to host his own television series."

"Huh." Earl turned to Gloria, a twinkle in his eye. "I guess we'll be seeing a lot more of Montague Black."

Chapter Two

Earl saw Pastor Benton again Friday. He had made the appointment before all the excitement in the press, so that morning he called to make sure the pastor was still available.

He didn't want either Gloria or Jenny to know about the visit, so he had to bite the expense and call for a cab. When the driver got to Earl's home, it took some doing for the cabbie to get his passenger situated in the car and the wheelchair folded and deposited in the trunk. Once they reached their destination, the driver had to dig the wheelchair back out of the trunk, figure out how to unfold it and lock it to Earl's satisfaction, and then get Earl back in the chair.

Then Earl had the challenge of entering the church building. He was accustomed to a greeter helping with the door every Sunday. But this was a weekday.

He finally managed his way into the lobby

and wheeled himself to the service elevator. He was actually several minutes late by the time he got to Pastor Benton's office.

"I have an appointment," he told the receptionist. "With Pastor Benton."

The woman smiled in a vacant way. "Make yourself comfortable, won't you? I'll let the pastor know you're here."

Earl parked next to a small table with several publications arranged on top. He grabbed an issue of a devotional magazine and fumbled with the pages. He tried to read, but the butterflies in his stomach had all his attention. Finally, he gave up and occupied himself with staring blankly out the window.

After forever, Pastor Benton appeared. "Hello, Earl! Come on in."

Hands trembling, Earl grabbed the rims of his wheels and pushed toward the inner office. His heart pounded in his ears.

"Sorry for the wait there." Pastor Benton took his chair, putting his elbows on his perfectly straightened desk. "I was on the phone with another media outlet. Ever since that sermon hit the Internet, the phone's been ringing off the hook."

"If you're busy, I can always come back."

"Nonsense! The flock always comes first." Pastor Benton leaned back in the padded swivel chair. "Now, how do you like things here at the church? Is the Sunday morning class going well?"

"Absolutely." Earl wasn't prepared for this line of discussion, but he grabbed onto it like it was a life preserver. "I really appreciate the approach. That is, the fact that the class isn't designed to *recruit* new members, but to help us determine whether we belong here."

"Every part of the body of Christ has its place."

"Yes." Earl paused. "That's what Gloria says."

"Uh-huh." The pastor smiled. "And how are things with Gloria?"

There it was. The topic Earl was avoiding. Which was silly, since it was why he had come. "Um, fine."

"Uh-huh." The pastor waited for Earl to elaborate.

"That's sort of why I want to talk to you." Earl turned his attention to his hands. "I don't rightly know how to go about this. When I think of all the years I wasted being angry at God . . ." He looked up at Pastor Benton. "Gloria helped me through that. Her and Jenny. If they both hadn't reached out to me, I'd probably still be curled up in my dark space."

"Tell me about your relationship with Gloria."

"We met out at the Candlewick Retirement Center. We were both residents until the place was shut down. Apparently, there were some state inspectors —"

The pastor nodded. "You told me all this. And, of course, you came to stay with us."

Earl smiled. "And I'll always be grateful for your hospitality, opening your home to a stranger like that."

"So where do things stand with you and Gloria now?"

Earl hesitated but finally spit it out. "I want to propose."

The pastor's eyebrows went up. "Really? That's great!"

Earl glanced up sheepishly. "Is it?"

"Why wouldn't it be?"

"I don't know. I'm just . . ." He didn't know how to end the sentence.

"You're both mature adults. And God has brought the two of you together. I saw that right away." He narrowed his eyes. "And you couldn't have ended up with a finer woman."

"Don't I know it." Earl put his hands on his lap. "When I lost my Barbara all those years ago, it never occurred to me I would ever be in love again."

"I understand." The phone rang, and the pastor started to reach for it then stopped himself. "I'll let Sadie get that."

Earl pointed. "I guess the phone *has* been ringing off the hook, huh? From what you said on Sunday about that psychic guy?"

The pastor frowned. "Afraid so."

"But I don't get it — what's the big deal? If the fella wants to help, and he has this gift, what's the harm?"

"The Bible makes it very clear that God has no patience with these kinds. 'Thou shalt not suffer not a witch to live.' "

"You said that on Sunday. But this guy hasn't been turning anyone into toads or anything. Not that I heard."

"Anyone who fools around with the supernatural, no matter how noble or innocent their intentions seem — unless they are directly working to the glory of God, there's only one other place that power can come from."

"Jenny said something like that, too."

"You better believe it. Ephesians 6:12 says, 'For we wrestle not against flesh and blood, but against principalities, against powers, against the rulers of the darkness of this world, against spiritual wickedness in high places.' "

"So, that's it, then? We just write this guy

off, and the police should refuse his help?"

"Best case, this man's a con artist preying on the weak and the desperate."

Earl raised one eyebrow. "And the worst case?"

"That this man really does wield some power — and he gets that power from the pit of hell."

As they wrapped up their meeting, Pastor Benton counseled Earl to simply talk to Gloria about his feelings. "The longer you keep something like this bottled up," the pastor said, "the worse it is for both of you."

When Earl got home, he called Gloria. Her voice sounded glad to hear from him. "How are you today?"

"I'm, uh, doing okay." He made a mental note to keep the stammering to a minimum. He took a deep breath. "Anyway, I wanted to ask you to dinner. And not at Skipper Dan's — someplace nice. Just the two of us."

"Really?" There was a pause.

Earl got nervous. "Is that all right?"

"Oh, yes. It's just . . ." There was another pause. When she spoke again, her voice trembled. "What's the occasion?"

"Oh . . ." Earl stopped, wondering whether he'd already said too much. "I just thought it might be nice."

"Where are we going?"

"It's a . . . surprise." Earl made a mental note that he still needed to think of a place. They set a time for her to pick him up and got off the phone.

He immediately grabbed the phone book and flipped to the restaurant listings. "Italian" sounded like a romantic choice, and Maggiano's sounded authentic.

It would be a good five hours before she'd show up. Plenty of time for him to pick out his clothes, brush his dentures, and spend the remaining four hours stewing over what he'd say to her.

Gloria arrived promptly at four thirty. They hoped to beat the dinner rush.

At Gloria's car, she got Earl into the passenger seat and the wheelchair into the trunk. She was an old hand at it by now. Once she got into the driver's seat, she turned and grinned. "So, where to?"

"I thought we'd go to Maggiano's."

"That sounds nice. How do we get there?"

Earl's eyes widened. "Um . . . I forgot to get directions." He tugged at his seat belt. "I should have called ahead."

"You didn't make a reservation?"

"Should I have?"

Gloria jangled her keys in thought. "I

guess we could call now. Do you have their number?"

Earl stuck his thumb in the direction of the apartment. "It's in the book. I guess I could . . ." He tugged at his seat belt again and tried to calculate the ordeal of getting back out, going back in, coming back to the car. . . .

"I can look it up — if you don't mind." She gave him a reassuring smile. "It just seems easier."

"I guess it would be." Earl gave Gloria his apartment key and told her where to find the phone book. He tried his best to hide his humiliation.

Gloria returned after several minutes. She fastened her seat belt then handed him the directions. "You'll have to be my navigator."

"And the reservations?"

"They said they don't take reservations."

Earl sighed. "I'm so embarrassed. I should have made that call."

Gloria, hands on the wheel, turned for the parking lot exit. "Don't worry about it, hon. It happens."

It took them about twenty minutes to get to the restaurant. They didn't talk much on the way, just Gloria reading off the occasional road sign and Earl reading her scribbled directions aloud.

Earl's stomach was in knots. He had spent all day mulling over what he might say to Gloria: how he'd broach the subject, how he'd explain himself, how he hoped she'd react. Despite having had several hours to think about it, Earl was no closer to knowing what those words were going to be.

When they reached their final turn, Earl the navigator called it too late, and Gloria had to circle the block. As they eventually pulled into the parking lot, Earl took some comfort in the thought that at least they'd have a nice Italian dinner.

But once inside, Earl's heart fell. Under dizzying colored lights children were scampering everywhere, from the video arcade to the playroom. The few grown-ups he could see were either racing after the kids or collapsing at their plastic tables.

The hostess approached. "Welcome to Maggiano's Family Fun Time Emporium!"

Earl stared. "I thought this was an Italian restaurant."

"No, but we do have all the spaghetti you can eat on Tuesdays." The woman clapped her hands together. "You folks bring your grandchildren tonight?"

"Um, no." Earl turned to Gloria. "Is this all right?"

"I'm sure it's fine."

Earl turned back to the hostess. "Just the two of us."

The hostess gave him a look and grabbed two menus. "Follow me." She led them to a square plastic table in the middle of the noisy dining area.

Earl looked around. "I was hoping for something more private."

The hostess let out a huff and snapped the menus back off the table. "This way." She led them to the far side of the big room, to a table against the fake brick wall. The table was smack dab next to the swinging kitchen door.

Earl was afraid to make any more requests. "This is great. Thank you."

When they were alone — more or less — Earl took refuge behind his menu. All the entrees had thematic names along the lines of "Walk the Plank Lasagna," "Pirate Parrot Pasta," and "Skull and Crossbones Meatballs."

He peeked over his menu at the back of Gloria's menu — it was embossed with a big crab holding salad tongs. Salad tongs? Her big red hairdo towered over the top. He told the back of her menu, "I expected something different."

"It's fine." She peeked around to give him a smile then returned to her menu. "It's nice to be alone for a change."

Earl had his mind on his agenda for the evening. "Uh-huh."

"I mean, I like Jenny. She's a lovely girl."

"Of course." He looked up. "But I guess I have a confession to make. The reason that we're almost never alone is that sometimes I'm . . . afraid."

She put out a hand and squeezed his arm. "What is there to be afraid of?"

Earl rubbed the back of his head. "Listen, Gloria, I'm not good at this kind of stuff. I'm not the smartest man. . . ."

"You're plenty smart!"

"Please." He cleared his throat and tried again. "Gloria, there comes a time in a man's life when he must face the —" He stopped because the waiter showed up.

The man set two glasses of water on the table. "Did you get a chance to look at the menu?"

"Sure," Earl said. He looked at Gloria. "Go ahead."

"I'll have the chopped steak."

The waiter took out a pad and pencil and scribbled. "The Swiss Armada Chopped Steak. And fries with that?"

"What other kinds of potatoes do you have?"

"Just the fries."

"What other vegetables?"
"Just the fries."
"All right then."
"So you want the fries?"
"Yes, please."
"And you, sir?"
"I'll have the spaghetti special that the hostess mentioned."
The waiter pursed his lips, shaking his head. "I don't think we have a spaghetti special."
"Something about all you can eat."
"Oh — that's only on Tuesdays."
"Huh." Earl thought about opening up his menu again then decided against it. "You know, I'll just have what she's having."
"Do you want the fries?"
"What other —" Earl stopped himself. "Of course. The fries."
The waiter left with their orders. Earl took a big gulp out of his water glass then wiped his mouth with the napkin. "So, as I was saying . . ."
"Excuse me," the waiter broke in, "but I forgot to ask you folks what you want to drink."
Gloria asked, "Do you have fruit tea?"
"We have iced tea."
"Sweetened or unsweetened?"

The waiter shrugged. "Iced tea."

"Fine, I'll have some iced tea."

Earl said, "The same."

After the waiter left, Earl found his courage starting to ebb. Trying to ignore the sound of children squealing in the background, he started over. "This morning, I went to see Pastor Benton."

She frowned. "How did you get out there?"

"I took a cab."

"I had this morning off. Why didn't you ask me to take you?"

"I didn't want to be a burden."

"Oh. Well. What'd y'all talk about?"

Earl felt his face turning red. "So, the pastor has been getting a lot of calls since his sermon was on TV. I guess with this psychic guy getting so much press, an angry preacher pounding his fist on the pulpit makes for good drama."

"I guess."

The waiter set down their iced teas. "One for you, and one for you." He raised his voice over the growing noise. More families with screaming kids were arriving by the minute. "We'll have your dinners for you soon."

After the waiter left again, Earl tried to remember where he left off. "So, um, the pastor and I talked a bit about this psychic business. I just figured that if a person can't help the police —"

"You can help."

Earl was taken aback. "Help what?"

"You can help the police catch this killer."

Earl gave her a cockeyed smile. "Don't be silly."

"You solved the murder of George Kent."

"That was just common sense. Anyone could have done it."

"But *you* did it." Gloria stood. "Will you excuse me?"

"Oh, of course." Earl pushed on his armrests to raise himself off the chair. It was a small gesture, but it was the best he could do.

Earl stared at the table. He looked at his plasticware and realized he didn't even have a fork; he had one of those half-fork/half-spoon dealies. What did they call that, a *"spork"?*

He sighed. The evening was not going well. His heart was so full, and he wanted so much to share it with Gloria. But the restaurant turned out to be all weird, and now the noisy crowd just kept getting noisier.

The kitchen door swung wide open, and the waiter was suddenly at their table. "Two plates of Swiss Armada Chopped Steak with french fries. Let me know if you need anything else."

After he left, Earl looked at the next table. Some man had a plate of fish. Earl leaned over. "Excuse me, what is that you got?"

The man seemed irked to be interrupted. "It's tortilla-crusted fish."

"Looks good."

"That's why I ordered it."

Earl looked down at his chopped steak. He wished he'd ordered the tortilla-crusted fish. Cutting up his meat, Earl braced himself for the conversation. *What do I want to say? What do I want out of this relationship?*

He was starting to wonder whether it would be better to wait for another time, another place. Until Gloria returned, he didn't even notice that he had started eating.

"I see our dinners came."

Earl looked up, down at his plate, and stopped chewing. "Umf smfy." He swallowed. "I didn't mean to start eating before you got back."

She took her chair. "That's all right."

"I was sort of lost in thought . . . and I didn't, um, realize I'd started."

"Don't worry about it, sweetie." She

picked up her plastic spork and knife and tried to cut her chopped steak. "I understand."

"I feel so awkward tonight." He put down his plasticware. "Life was so much simpler when I was miserable."

"What's the matter, darlin'?" She squeezed his arm again. "By the way, what were you saying earlier?"

"Oh, um . . ." Earl cleared his throat. "Gloria, there comes a time in a man's life —"

A chirping sound came from Gloria's purse. She reached inside for her cell phone and frowned when she saw the number. "It's a call from the church."

"This time of night?"

"It's the prayer hotline. I need to take this." She got up, Earl lifted himself off his wheelchair, and she smiled at him as she left the table to find a quiet spot.

While she was gone, Earl wondered whether to continue eating his chopped steak. In the end, he decided to just sit back and wait. He wasn't very hungry anyway.

If only he could find the words to say to Gloria. If only he could figure out how to speak his heart.

After several minutes, Gloria returned. Earl asked, "So, what was that all about?"

"Pastor Benton and that psychic are going to have a meeting tomorrow morning. And the group wants everyone to pray about it."

"So the two are getting together to talk things out? Maybe bury the hatchet?" Earl chuckled. "I guess as long as one of 'em don't try burying the hatchet in the other man's head."

Gloria sniffed. "I can't imagine the pastor intends to do *that.*"

Unable to think of a reply, Earl simply nodded.

Returning to her chopped steak, Gloria asked in a playful voice, "So, what were you saying? You know, earlier . . . ?"

Earl let out a sigh. He looked over at the fish on the next table. "I wish I'd ordered that."

Chapter Three

After that last interruption at dinner, Earl had lost his nerve altogether. They spent the rest of the evening talking about little things.

The meeting between Pastor Andrew Benton and celebrated psychic channelist Montague Black was set for the next morning. They were going to meet at Heritage Care — the site of the most recent death.

According to the morning paper, the Fletcher County Sheriff's Department was still officially investigating the death of Cloris Thomas, unwilling to categorize it as a "murder." Nonetheless, "sources close to the investigation" claimed there was evidence somebody had been in the room of the victim the night she died. These same "sources" also said it was Black who brought this evidence to the attention of investigators.

Saturday morning, Gloria showed up at

Earl's apartment to drive him to the meeting. He was exhausted; he hadn'tslept all night. "Explain to me again, why do we have to get involved?"

"Because our pastor's going into the lion's den. We need to show our support and pray protection around him."

"Can't we pray from here? There could be a lot of yelling. I don't like conflict."

"How can you say that? You're one of the most contrary men I know."

"Yes, but my form of contrariness takes the form of not getting involved."

"What was that when George Kent died? You certainly got involved there."

Earl grunted. "And look how that turned out."

She put her hands on her hips. "What are you scared of? Come on, what's the worst that could happen?"

Not feeling like he had much choice, Earl relented.

The drive to Heritage Care was uneventful, if long. As they drove farther and farther off the main road, Gloria squinted out the windshield at the passing trees. "I wonder why it has to be all the way out here?"

"Maybe that psychic person wants to be close to the vibrations or something." Earl looked at Gloria. Her red hair glistened as the sunlight streamed through the car windows. She flashed a smile at Earl and turned her eyes back to the curvy road.

Earl felt those butterflies in his stomach again. He wanted so much to resolve the question of their relationship. For good or bad, just get the question answered and done with. But he needed to work up his nerve again.

They drove on a bit more in silence. He watched the little pine-tree-shaped dealie swing on her rearview mirror. Finally he cleared his throat. "Hey, um . . ."

After a pause, she glanced in his direction then back at the road. "Yes?"

"You know, we never got to finish our conversation last night."

"We didn't?"

"No." Earl watched more trees pass his window. He noticed the scent of her perfume.

"Why, what were we talking about?"

They came upon a bunch of cars in front of them — many with out-of-state license plates — all headed in the same direction. Gloria tapped her brakes as she got close to the last car in the line.

Earl coughed. "Never mind. We'll talk about it later."

"If that's what you want."

The caravan continued along the country road. Earl wondered what these fellas were meeting for, anyway. What was this meeting supposed to prove?

When they reached the rural address, the parking lot was jam-packed. All the official parking spaces were occupied, and several cars had squeezed into a lot of nonspaces. Now cars were lining up haphazardly along the road.

Gloria squeezed in beside a van marked as an official news vehicle. The tight fit added some difficulty to getting Earl out his passenger door and into his wheelchair. But eventually they worked it out and made their way across the gravel parking lot toward the entrance.

The sun in his eyes, Earl squinted at the small group gathered under the awning. He glanced at Gloria. "There seems to be quite a crowd."

With some twists and turns, accompanied by the occasional "Excuse us" and "Pardon me," they managed to navigate his wheelchair through the cluster, enter the glass double doors, and make it into the lobby. Inside, they found an even bigger crowd, practically shoulder to shoulder.

Nearly everyone was separated into similarly dressed cliques. Some were well-dressed, others were casually dressed, while others wore costumes and weird clothing. Some seemed young and hopeful, others old and fearful. One huddle of youngsters in black chanted, while a girl tapped a musical triangle at deliberate intervals. Another group was dressed in brown cloaks, their hoods pulled over their heads.

Earl grunted. "What's going on with those people?"

Gloria furrowed her brow. "Which ones?"

"Over there in the robes."

"I guess they like to wear robes." She waved to their right. "I see our group over there."

"Wonderful." Earl squinted in their direction. Some faces seemed familiar, including a few from his new-members' class. He made an effort to put on a pleasant face.

Also among the group was their young friend, Jenny, who waved back. "Mr. Walker! Mrs. Logan!" She had to yell over the noise in the lobby. "Glad you two made it!"

"Thanks, College," Earl said as they drew close. He gave her a wry smile. "Gloria put up a real fight, but I convinced her that it was important to come out this morning."

Jenny and Gloria both laughed, but a young man next to Jenny frowned. "It's very important to show our support to Pastor

Benton. These are dark times."

Gloria smiled politely. "Um, yes. You're right."

Jenny turned to the serious young man. "Mr. Walker was teasing."

"Oh, really?" The young man stroked his goatee as if he'd actually been told something quite weighty. His manner got on Earl's nerves. Earl hoped College wasn't falling for this one.

Eyes wandering the room, Earl saw a well-dressed man making the rounds. He was in his forties, in a dark purple suit, striped white shirt, and red tie. His short brown hair and beard were immaculately trimmed.

The man stopped at a group of older people. Earl gripped the rims of the wheels on his chair and pushed himself in their direction.

"I apologize for any inconvenience, I assure you," he heard the man in the purple suit saying. The man turned to a woman in a flowered housecoat that had seen better days. "So, you're sure you haven't seen Mr. Black?"

All the old heads shook, and the man was off. Earl moved himself closer. "What was that all about?"

A man in a blue bathrobe, leaning on a walker, looked down at Earl. "He says he's the psychic feller."

"That's not what he said, Peyton," the woman in the housecoat said. "He's the man's manager."

A nurse appeared. "Now, you folks are supposed to stay back in the residential area."

Earl turned and wheeled himself the other direction before he got caught in the herd. With all the people milling around him, he couldn't see his group from church, so he started making his way toward the right.

A man and a woman burst out of the hall. Earl recognized the man as celebrated "psychic channelist" Montague Black. The man wore a black suit and white shirt buttoned all the way to the collar, but no tie. "Stop following me! There is nothing left to say!"

The woman, in a dark blue pantsuit and carrying a clipboard, had trouble keeping up with him. "Please, Monty! Just give us another chance! I know we could still —"

"I'm done talking about this!" Black whirled on her. Startled, she dropped her purse, its contents spilling on the floor. He shouted, "If I'd known you were behind this, I would have refused! You put this whole thing together just to get to me!" He stormed off.

"Monty Schwartz! Don't you walk away from me like that!" The woman knelt to pick up her things. As Black faded into the crowd, she called out, "If I can't have you, no one can! You'll be sorry! I'll —" She stopped suddenly, noticing the people watching. She grabbed the rest of the items — compact, key ring, pens, candy — and shoved it all back into her bag. She stood, composed herself, and strode off.

Earl turned to a man holding a big video camera. "What was that all about?"

"That's Sheree Jackson, the activities director here. I guess they were an item or something."

"Huh. Thanks." Earl turned again to find his church group. He decided that if he just followed the wall, he'd eventually reach them. He stopped when he came upon something on the floor. It was a wrapped piece of candy. Ms. Jackson must have lost it when the contents of her purse spilled out.

Jenny appeared in the crowd. "Mr. Walker! Are you okay?"

"Yeah, I was just checking the place out."

She asked in a low voice, "How are things with Gloria?"

"What?" Earl jumped in his chair, craning his neck to make sure Gloria wasn't anywhere nearby. Then he relaxed, feeling himself blush. "Unfortunately, there's not much to report. Last night, I tried to bring up the subject of our, you know, relationship. But we got interrupted." He squinted up at Jenny. "Do you know anything about Maggiano's?"

"The place with all the noisy games?"

"Hmm. I expected something different." Earl shifted in his chair.

They neared the front entrance, where more people were forcing their way in. One of them called to Jenny and came over. They started a conversation.

Earl tried again to get his bearings. With the crowd, it was hard from his low vantage point to see across the room. Putting his hands to the wheels again, he took note of the lobby's structure. From the front doors, the angled walls of the lobby pushed outward. There was a hall on the far left, two doors in the wall facing him, the doors to the elevator, an open staircase, and then another hall on the far right.

As Earl weaved in and out of the crowd, he overheard bits of conversations. Based on what little he could hear, the various people smashed into the lobby included supporters for Pastor Andrew Benton and for the church in general; supporters for psychic Montague Black and for the psychic world in general; plus assorted religious leaders, political leaders, observers, onlookers, reporters, and bloggers, not to mention a mass of skeptics, Trekkies, Wiccans, gamers, Jedis, New Agers, and other assorted fruits and nuts. Earl even thought he saw a couple of Elvis impersonators.

More than one camera crew roamed the lobby, taking note of the various factions in attendance. Earl tried his best to stay off camera.

The flow of foot traffic somehow maneuvered him to the left of the lobby. Making his way along the far left wall, Earl looked down the hall that bordered the lobby. That woman from before, Ms. Jackson, the one who chased Black into the lobby, seemed to be getting chewed out by a bald man in a brown suit. She shivered, her arms folded.

Turning to avoid them, Earl wheeled himself to the wall at the back of the lobby and rolled toward the door to the first room. As he neared the open doorway, Montague Black shot out, followed by a burly man in a black shirt, head shaved, his arms thick as logs. He jabbed a finger at Black. "You can't pull out now! That will botch the whole deal!"

Black tried to brush him off. "Not my

problem."

"You already agreed to be part of this! I got the advance and everything!"

"Take it up with my manager." Black, not seeing Earl, tripped on the wheelchair and stumbled. He glared at Earl then looked down the hall. Apparently not wanting to encounter Ms. Jackson again, he turned and pushed past the burly man. "Talk to my manager about it."

"You better do right by me!" the burly man growled and went back into the room. The official sign said LIBRARY, but a piece of paper taped next to it said MEDIA.

Earl peeked inside. Long tables were set up around the walls, and all manner of folks were set up with their computers and their telephones and their cameras and cables and such. The back wall was a series of floor-to-ceiling windows, the sunlight streaming in. Blocking the glass sliding doors was a long, covered table offering coffee, soda, and plates of cookies and crackers. The room bustled as men and woman ran around checking their computers and making calls on cell phones.

This seemed to be where the action was. Earl wheeled inside the door, but thick cables strung across the carpet made it difficult for his wheelchair to go any farther.

In one corner of the room, the burly man shuffled assorted papers and stuffed them into his bag. He slung the bag onto a table then stomped past Earl, out the door.

Earl spoke to the nearest person, a woman typing on her laptop. "What's up with that guy?"

She looked up from her screen, blinking. "What guy?"

"The big guy in the black T-shirt. He could be a pro wrestler."

"Oh! That's Hamilton Page. He writes true-crime books."

"And what about the guy in the purple suit?"

"Huh? Oh, that'd be Jack Carpenter. He's Black's manager." She smiled weakly and turned back to her typing. "Excuse me, I have to file this."

Earl turned to leave and saw Pastor Benton across the room, talking with a silver-haired man in a gray suit. The other man was holding a microphone, and a slovenly guy standing just behind him was aiming a big video camera at Pastor Benton.

Earl strained to hear what the pastor was saying. "The devil often tempts people with a shortcut — that's what he offered Jesus in the wilderness. 'There is a way which seemeth right unto a man, but the end thereof are the ways of death.' Mankind wants the easy way; we want the shortcut. But God does things in the correct way and in the correct time. And He is infinite, He is eternal, His ways are not our ways. But tiny, finite, mortal men and women have a tendency to be spiritually lazy and embrace the shortcut — and often they pay the price for that."

The man with the microphone said, "Sounds like the proverbial 'If it sounds too good to be true, it probably is.' "

Earl didn't hear the pastor's reply, because there was suddenly a hand on his shoulder. He looked up and saw manager Jack Carpenter, in all his purple-suited glory. The man said, "I was assured that all the residents would be kept out of our hair!"

"Hey! I'm not a resident!"

"Well, you can't be in here. Unless you have a media badge," the man sneered. "Do you have a media badge? No? Then you're going to have to leave."

"Fine." Earl turned to exit, but a young woman blocked the doorway. She started yelling in two languages, poking Carpenter in the chest. "Where is that weasel hiding?"

Carpenter backed up defensively. "Divina, this is neither the time nor the place."

"Neither of you *idiotas tienes el nervio* to

take my calls — and when I found him here, he ran away!"

"I handle Montague's business dealings. I'm sorry I didn't return your calls yet, but I've been tied up setting up this event. Next week, we'll sit down —"

"We talk about this today! He signed a contract!"

He sighed. "Fine. We'll talk. After the meeting. Trust me, I'll handle it."

"I will not let him ruin me! I will keel him first!" She stared at Carpenter a second, her rage barely contained. Then she turned and left, a string of Spanish curses blistering the air behind her.

Earl raised an eyebrow. "Who was that?"

"Divina Zuniga, the producer for —" He looked down at Earl. "I told you to leave."

"But she was in my way. How do you expect me to —"

Suddenly, Hamilton Page, the enormous man with the shaved head, reappeared. "Hey, what's going on? Your boy refuses to —"

Carpenter frowned. "Not now."

"I have a deadline to meet! I tried to talk to Black out in the lobby —"

"I'm the business manager. You talk to me about this."

"Then you have an obligation to —"

"Look, I'm tied up right now, but we'll talk about this right after Montague and the reverend have their meeting. Trust me, this is not a problem. I'll handle it."

Page stared back a second. Finally, he growled, "You'd better," and stormed off.

Earl barely noticed Pastor Benton had approached until he felt the hand on his shoulder. "Hello, Earl," the pastor said, grinning. "So, what do you think?"

Carpenter cut in. "Reverend Benton? I'm Jack Carpenter, the manager for Montague Black."

The pastor was stoically polite. "Hello."

"If we could have a few minutes, I would like to coordinate this event for maximum coverage. I'm sure it could generate some great synergy for both our camps."

"I'll tell ya," the pastor said, eyes turning to the crowded lobby behind him, "when y'all set up this meeting, I expected something more private. You know, just a meeting of the minds."

Carpenter blinked. "There must be some mistake. I'm sure that you mean —" He stopped himself, his eyes looking somewhere else for a second. Then he shook it off and spoke to the pastor again. "Once this meeting was set up, it provided too great an opportunity to pass up. It only makes sense to get as much as we can out of this. Now, if we could plan . . ."

"Actually," Pastor Benton said, motioning across the lobby, "I really need a few minutes with my flock."

"Your . . . ?"

"My church family."

"Oh — of course!" The man was clearly rattled but was pressing through. "Shall we say, ten minutes?"

"Um, I suppose so."

The manager nodded curtly and shot off on a mission. Pastor Benton and Earl headed for their group, Earl taking quick glances over his shoulder.

The door to the second room opened. Black came out, and Carpenter lurched in his direction. Whatever it was that Carpenter was saying, his body language did not indicate it was polite. Black waved him off and went back into the room. Carpenter followed him.

Pastor Benton stopped at a group of men and women in suits. Earl heard some of them speak to the pastor in warm, familiar tones.

After several minutes, the pastor started off again. Earl followed. "Tell me something, Pastor," he said. "Let's say this Montague Black character really does get his information from the devil. Why is it that Black is helping, but you can't?"

"I don't understand. What do you —"

"If you have a pipeline to God, why doesn't He at least have the same information for the police? If not more? Come to think of it, what about all the other preachers who represent God?"

The pastor stopped a second, thinking. "First of all, Earl, we don't know what this Black person has really done. We only know what they say in the news. Maybe they're misreporting it for the sake of a story. We don't know."

"All the same —"

"Besides, we don't know everything that goes on in the spiritual realm. We don't see what God and His angels are doing."

"Fine." Earl's shoulders slumped. As they continued across the lobby, Earl looked around. Carpenter was roaming the lobby, frequently checking his watch.

The elevator doors opened, and the Hispanic woman, Divina Zuniga, came out. Carpenter went up to her and whispered in her ear. She nodded and went to the second room. Meanwhile, Carpenter stopped someone and compared his watch with theirs.

Earl turned back to Pastor Benton and saw how far he'd fallen behind. It was tricky trying to maneuver a wheelchair through a crowd of milling, pacing people.

Someone almost backed into Earl, and he had to stop. "Hey!"

The kid was surprised to see him. "Sorry, old man!"

Earl grimaced. "It's fine." He bit his lip before he said something else.

Suddenly, the nurse appeared again. "There you are! I *thought* I lost one from before. Do you need me to help wheel you back there, sir?"

Earl shrunk back. "What? What are you talking about?"

"Now, sir, you know that residents of the nursing home are supposed to stay out of here this morning. It's for your own safety."

"But I don't live here," Earl growled. "I'm with those people over there!"

"Now, now." She grabbed the handles on the back of Earl's chair and started pushing him after the others. "Here, let me just —"

"College! Hey, College!" Earl waved his hand for Jenny's attention. "Help me!"

Even with Earl fighting the nurse the whole way — she was stronger than she looked — she managed to push his chair past the elevator, past the staircase. They got all the way to the edge of the hall before Jenny could catch up. "What's the matter,

Mr. Walker?"

"Would you tell this militant woman that I don't live here?"

"Yes, ma'am, Mr. Walker's with us." Jenny waved a hand toward their group in the far corner. "We're all from Pastor Benton's church."

The nurse hesitated. "If you say so . . ." She reluctantly walked away, glancing back once, twice, before she disappeared down the hall.

Earl let out a big breath. "Whew! That was closer than I like it."

He gripped the rims of his wheels and started off again. He glanced back. Hamilton Page came down the stairs, clearly still agitated. Carpenter went up to him and spoke with him briefly. He pointed to the door of the second room. Checking his watch again, Carpenter stopped someone and asked the time.

Earl caught up with Pastor Benton and the group of familiar faces. The pastor had to raise his voice above the din. "Praise God! I'm thrilled y'all came out. I certainly appreciate your prayers and your support."

Gloria was beaming. Jenny was intent. The serious young man furrowed his brow, stroking his goatee. "What are your intentions with this meeting?"

"I'm just here to represent the Lord." Pastor Benton looked at the noisy crowd pressing in. "However, I was not expecting such a public event."

"Not too much of a surprise," Earl grumbled to himself. "When you're meeting with someone as desperate for the spotlight as that man."

Pastor Benton nodded. "You know, Earl, I think you're absolutely right."

Earl was embarrassed. He didn't think anybody would hear his comment.

Black's manager, Carpenter, approached. "Reverend?" He looked at his watch. "What time do you have?"

Several in the circle looked at their watches, including Pastor Benton. Earl looked at his wrist. He really needed to get a watch.

Pastor Benton said, "I have ten minutes to eleven."

"Okay, then, I guess Montague is ready for you now."

"Right now? But we're not scheduled until —"

Carpenter shrugged apologetically. "We had to move the schedule around a little. As it was, I hoped to speak to you beforehand, but that's how it goes. If you could just go right in . . . ?"

Pastor Benton looked around at the others. Finally, he said, "Fine. I guess that'll be fine."

"Thank you." Carpenter motioned for him to lead the way.

Pastor Benton looked back at the group, taking a minute to meet several sets of eyes. "Pray that God's will be done."

Some in the group replied, "Amen."

Pastor Benton pushed through the gauntlet of reporters brandishing microphones, flashing bulbs, and video cameras. When he reached the second door, Carpenter opened it for him and stepped aside.

Pastor Benton went in. Carpenter closed the door then walked back toward the front of the lobby. "If I can please have everyone's attention!" The rumbling died as all eyes turned in his direction. He checked his watch. "After Mr. Black and Reverend Benton have a chance to speak privately, they'll make a joint statement to the public and to the press."

A low murmur percolated throughout the lobby. The crowd pressing around them, Gloria said to Jenny, "I still can't believe all these people who showed up."

Earl grumped, "I guess the prospect of a fistfight between a celebrity psychic and a small-town pastor is too good to pass up."

He turned to Gloria. "So the pastor is in there, and we're out here. What happens now?"

The woman next to her said, "Shall we join hands?"

The prayer group, twenty people strong, formed a circle. If anyone other than Gloria and Jenny had been on either side of Earl, he'd have refused to hold hands. He glanced self-consciously over his shoulder at the others in the lobby, but they were occupied with their own activities.

Head bowed and eyes closed, the woman started the prayer. "Heavenly Father," she said aloud, "we pray for Your will to be done here today, and that Your Kingdom and Your name be glorified. We rebuke those powers which would work against Your purposes."

It all sounded mighty highfalutin' to Earl. But he guessed these folks were more practiced at talking to God than he was.

"Please be glorified by these proceedings. And we just pray a hedge of protection around Pastor Benton this morning."

A *"hedge"* of protection? Couldn't they ask for something sturdier?

As the prayer continued, several members of the circle added their own words in turn. Earl followed along silently; he understood most of the words, but not in this context or combined in these ways.

He peeked up, glancing around the room. Carpenter stood by the front entrance. The spurned pant-suited woman, Sheree Jackson, was in the hall, unwrapping a piece of candy and popping it in her mouth. The burly man, Hamilton Page, paced by the elevator. The Hispanic woman, Divina Zuniga, talked with a cameraman by the staircase.

Earl closed his eyes again as the prayer continued. Without a watch, Earl had no idea how much time passed. Ten minutes? Twenty? All he knew is that the prayer broke off was midsentence when the door swung open.

Pastor Benton stood in the doorway. He stared at the room, jaw set, hands at his sides, clenching and unclenching into fists. Finally, he seemed to gather himself together and then marched across the lobby. The reporters pounced, shouting, jabbing microphones and cameras at him.

Carpenter looked puzzled. "Wait! What about your joint statement? Where's Black?" He started walking toward the meeting room.

Ignoring the reporters, Pastor Benton just walked past the prayer group on the way out. He grumbled, "I'm getting out of here."

Jenny followed him. "What happened?"

Earl glanced toward the open door behind him — the psychic still hadn't come out of the room. Earl turned back to the pastor, who was nearing the exit.

A shout cut across the room. "He's been stabbed! Call the police!"

Everyone turned to see Jack Carpenter standing in the doorway to the meeting room, his face ashen. He pointed at the front entrance, where Pastor Benton had his hand on the door. "Grab that man! He just killed Montague Black!"

Earl turned to Gloria. "*This* is the worst that could happen!"

Chapter Four

There was some bit of chaos — shouting, crying, shoving. As one, the crowd pressed in on Pastor Benton. Four or five men more or less tackled him at the door and dragged him back across the lobby to the meeting room.

Gloria clutched Earl's shoulder. "What does it mean?"

"I — I don't know." Earl frowned. "It has to be some kind of misunderstanding."

Carpenter was no longer in the doorway. While the crowd had rushed the pastor, Carpenter must have gone into the room to check on the victim. Folks now crowded the door as reporters tried to get their story. Other reporters ran to the media room to file what little they could.

After some minutes, medical personnel — Earl had to assume they were on staff at Heritage Care — pushed through the crowd, yelling, shoving their way inside the room. Pastor Benton had not reappeared since he was dragged back inside.

Ms. Jackson pulled a chair from against the wall and stood on it. "Everybody, please listen! We've called the sheriff. We ask that you remain on the premises until they have an opportunity to assess the situation. Thank you for your patience."

Earl wondered whether it was a good idea asking all these freaks to hang around. It was a good ten or fifteen minutes before he heard sirens — even the ambulance had to make its way along the winding country road. The EMTs rushed in, pushing their way through the crowded lobby to the fateful room. The door closed.

After several minutes, the door opened again. The white-jacketed EMTs came back out, wheeling the stretcher. It was empty. Nobody spoke as the men made their way to the exit and then out.

Earl moved closer to the window. As the EMTs put the stretcher back into the ambulance, a black-and-white squad car pulled up the drive. It parked right at the entrance. A brown sedan pulled in behind it.

Two uniformed men exited the first car. Earl recognized them as Sheriff Meyer and Deputy Fisher. Out of the second car came a third man in a wrinkled blue suit, wearing an outdated fedora, and a kid in a button-up shirt and jeans, carrying a large camera.

Gloria asked, "What do you think is going on?"

Earl shook his head absently. Finally, he mumbled, "I don't know."

As the sheriff came in the door, he blinked at the packed audience huddled in the lobby. "What's all this?"

Sheree Jackson pushed her way up to the sheriff. "Come this way, Sheriff. The body's in here."

Earl stiffened. Body? What had Pastor Benton gotten himself into?

The sheriff turned to Deputy Fisher behind him. "Why don't you start gettin' these folks' names and numbers?"

The deputy blinked. "All of them?"

"Of course." The sheriff turned to the man in the wrinkled suit and the kid with the camera. "Doc, Jimmy, y'all come with me." Following the woman, the three men disappeared into the meeting room.

Deputy Fisher raised his voice. "All right, folks, if you want to form a straight line . . ."

Everyone looked at each other then around the room. It was a big, angular room, everyone more or less shoulder to shoulder. Some brave soul cried out,

"Straight line where?"

The deputy, undaunted, replied in a loud voice, "A straight line right in front of me here." He headed to a spot to the left of the front door and pressed his back to the wall. He flipped open a notebook, clicked his pen, then turned to the nearest people, who happened to be the clique wearing the hooded robes. Earl would have given his dentures to know how they explained themselves.

Gloria pushed closer, next to Earl. Her eyes narrowed and she growled, "That man!"

It took him a second before he remembered the source of her hostility. Then he stifled a smile. "Aw, he's just doing his duty, Gloria." He glanced back at the meeting room again. What was going on in there?

Over the next hour or so, official-looking folks came and went. Who were they? What was their role here?

As the deputy catalogued everyone in the lobby, the crowd began to dwindle as folks were allowed to leave. Earl and the prayer circle waited their turns. Some prayed aloud over the situation, still not sure exactly what to pray for. As Deputy Fisher began collecting the names and contact information from the circle, they began drifting away, too.

When the deputy came to Gloria and Earl, there was a flicker of recognition in his eyes. But all the same, he asked their names and contact information.

When he got to Jenny, though, he stopped. "Hey! What are you doing here?"

She huffed. "We came out here to give our support to Pastor Benton."

"What?" The deputy's eyes widened. "He's here somewhere?"

Jenny nodded. "Didn't you know?"

He blushed. "I didn't get much chance to ask. The sheriff's got me taking down names."

Earl jabbed a thumb toward the closed door. "The pastor and that psychic fella had a meeting. We saw both men go in. So far, only the one has ever come out."

"Oh." The deputy's face darkened. "That's bad. That's very bad."

Gloria grew alarmed. "Why? What happened?"

"I don't know that I'm allowed to share anything at this point." The deputy regained his composure. "Besides, *I'm* supposed to be asking the questions. Now, um, Miss Jenny, I have to write down your number."

"You have my number."

He let out a breath. "I'm trying to be official here."

She stared at him a second then rattled off a phone number. He nodded, mumbled a thanks, looked at her, tried to say something, decided against it, and moved on to the next person. Jenny, Gloria, and Earl moved out of the way.

Gloria asked, “What was that all about?”

Jenny blushed. “We sort of went out.”

Earl’s eyebrows went up. “On a date?”

Gloria pointed toward the meeting room. “Look! Someone’s coming out!”

Sure enough, Sheriff Meyer had come out. He found Divina Zuniga and began talking to her.

Gloria bent to whisper into Earl’s ear, “What do you suppose they’re talking about?”

He shook his head. “I’m sure it’s an accident or a misunderstanding. You know how excited people get.”

Gloria said, “I don’t know. . . .”

Earl wheeled as close as he could, Gloria inching along with him. All he could catch was that Divina had created a syndicated television series that Montague Black was supposed to host next season. Now that Black was dead, she was out one TV show.

The sheriff, done with Ms. Zuniga, directed her to one of his deputies. The sheriff then moved on to the man in the purple suit, Jack Carpenter. They spoke in low tones.

Earl was straining to hear something when Gloria shouted, "It's Pastor Benton!" The pastor saw them and shambled over. Gloria hugged him. "Pastor, are you all right?"

His eyes seemed glazed. He asked in a shaky voice, "I guess the rest of the group's left? I suppose it's just as well."

Jenny asked, "What happened? What's going on?"

Pastor Benton found a chair against the wall and collapsed into it. "I don't know. I don't understand any of this."

"Well, what did you and that psychic talk about?"

"We didn't talk about" — the pastor shook his head slowly, like he was dazed — "anything."

"What, the two of you just stared at each other?" Earl glanced across the room. The sheriff had now moved on to the burly man, Hamilton Page. Earl turned back to the pastor. "Well, you must have done something. You were both in there for quite a while. If the two of you got into some kind of fight . . ." Earl squinted. "Unless he attacked you and got hurt in the scuffle."

The pastor put his face in his hands. Then

he looked up. "He wasn't in the room at all."

"What do you mean?"

"The room was empty."

Earl shifted in his wheelchair, craning his neck to look back toward the meeting room. He turned back to the pastor. "Are you saying that this Black fella is *missing?* Then why the ambulance and all that?"

The pastor stared vacantly at the front exit. Then he turned to Earl, locking eyes. "What did you see? From where you were sitting?"

Earl stared back. "I don't understand what you're asking. We were out here the whole time. The door was closed."

"Yes, but if there's something — anything — you might have seen . . . something unusual?"

Gloria moved closer to him. "What are you asking?"

The pastor reached over and gripped her arm. "Please. Any thing at all? It could mean the difference between life and . . . and . . ." He broke off.

Gloria nodded and fell back against the wall, her breathing labored. She slowly shook her head. "We came to pray over your meeting. We formed a circle when you went in. Susie Brown started praying first. She asked for wisdom, and for a spiritual breakthrough —"

"Yes, yes," the pastor cut her off. "What else?"

Gloria bit her lip. "I can't think of anything special. You went in the room, we prayed, you came back out. Then that man yelled something about somebody being stabbed."

Earl demanded, "Pastor, what's going on? They haven't explained anything. It's just been a bunch of ambulance workers and police and some kid with a camera —"

The pastor said to no one in particular, "I just don't understand what happened."

Earl leaned forward, locking eyes with the pastor. "What did the sheriff find in that room?"

Pastor Benton just shook his head.

Sheriff Meyer approached. "Reverend, I need to speak with you again, please."

Pastor Benton blinked at him. "Of course."

As the two walked away, Earl took note of the sheriff's posture. He was prepared to take any physical action necessary if his suspect — in this case, Pastor Andrew Benton — suddenly burst into fight or flight. They went by the door to the meeting room.

Gloria said, "I want to know what has the pastor so rattled. It can't be . . ." She let the sentence hang in the air.

Earl looked down at his hands. He was wringing them again. Without looking up, he told Gloria, "You know, when I went to see the pastor at his office, it wasn't to talk about church stuff."

"It wasn't?"

Earl shook his head, still afraid to look up. "No. The reason I went to talk to the pastor was —"

"Wait a second." Gloria was staring across the room.

Earl turned to see the sheriff call the deputy over. As the deputy stood by, the sheriff turned the pastor to the wall and frisked him. He must have felt something, because he grabbed a handkerchief from his own pocket, reached into the pastor's pocket, and pulled out something.

A letter opener — its blade stained brown.

The sheriff handed it to the deputy, his voice carrying. "Andrew Benton, you have the right to remain silent. . . ."

CHAPTER FIVE

Deputy Fisher handcuffed Pastor Benton and led him out to the squad car. Outside, Earl, Gloria, and Jenny stayed among those who watched the authorities wrap up the crime scene. The body was removed, the door to the meeting room shut, yellow tape stretched across the entrance.

The hearse drove away. The squad car followed, as did the brown sedan.

Earl glanced around. Nearly everyone had left. No more groupies, no more churchies, no more media. The few stragglers looked as shell-shocked as he felt.

He cleared his throat. "I guess we better get going."

For lack of a better plan, the three decided to go somewhere for lunch. It was not so much a question of them being hungry as much as a need to find a place to sit, to decompress, and to commiserate. And, if possible, to figure out what had happened to the world.

Earl was withdrawn as they got him into the car and put his wheelchair in the trunk. On the drive over, Gloria and Jenny tried some nervous chatter, something about knitting. He just stared out the window.

They ended up at a diner on the interstate. The parking lot was full, and inside there was a wait for a table. The hostess seemed surprised by the sudden influx of customers. Earl guessed that most everyone who had left Heritage Care had shown up at the diner.

As they waited for the hostess to call Earl's name, Gloria and Jenny took up the small talk again. Earl just looked around the congested waiting area, soaking in the details. Anything to keep his mind off the past few hours. However, despite his best efforts, flickers of memories kept intruding. Sheree Jackson shaking her fist. Divina Zuniga cursing in Spanish. Hamilton Page making threats.

Finally, Gloria and Jenny ran out of nothing to talk about. Fortunately, the hostess called for Mr. Walker's party, and they were led to a table. The ladies slid onto the benches on either side. Earl's wheelchair was pushed up as close to the edge of the table as he could get.

They were offered water and coffee and were given menus. Earl stared at his silverware. Particularly, the knife.

What could have possessed Pastor Benton to stab that man? And why keep the murder weapon in your pocket? If it had been Earl, he'd have never kept the knife with him.

But as Earl thought back to the scene, he remembered the pastor pushing for the exit. If he hadn't been stopped at the door, he could have been outside in seconds. Was he hoping to dispose of the murder weapon?

Gloria glumly stirred her coffee.

Earl cleared his throat. "A lot to take in, huh?"

Gloria's eyes snapped wide at him. "I just can't imagine it!" She looked down at her coffee, still stirring. "Someone so sweet . . ."

Earl grumped, "Well, he did get pretty heated about that psychic. He was pounding his fist on the podium Sunday."

Gloria sniffled. "That doesn't make him a killer!"

"But he was angry. When even a man of God gets angry . . ."

Jenny broke open a packet of sugar over her coffee. "Mr. Walker, the Bible says, 'Be ye angry, and sin not.' "

Earl squinted at her. "It does?"

"There's such a thing as righteous anger.

The Bible says Jesus got angry. The apostles got angry. There are times when God gets angry."

"Well . . ."

"The sin is not in the feeling; the sin's in how we act on it. We don't have license to abandon our Christian principles — the Bible calls us not to use our anger as an excuse to lose control."

Earl sat back in the wheelchair. "But that's the question, isn't it? Did the pastor lose control?"

Gloria shook her head. "I don't believe it!"

Earl averted his eyes. He tried to make his voice soft. "Look, I'm the first to admit that all this church stuff is new to me. But you have to look at this logically. The news is full of pastors who do all sorts of horrible things, sometimes in the name of God. Sometimes just for their own immoral reasons."

Jenny started to reply, but the waitress came to the table. The lady snapped her gum, asking, "What can we get y'all today?"

None of them had looked at their menus. Earl looked at the waitress. "You know, I haven't really decided yet. Why don't you start with them?"

Gloria flipped over her menu. She said to

Jenny, "Why don't you go ahead?"

Jenny, obviously still fuming, looked at her menu.

Finally, the waitress asked, "Would y'all like a couple more minutes?"

Earl tried his best to smile. "That'd be great."

After the waitress left, Jenny opened her mouth to speak, but Earl beat her to it. "I'm just saying, there are stories all the time about preachers who turn out bad — stealing money, cheating on their wives, running pyramid schemes —"

"We didn't say that all ministers everywhere do the work of God. The Bible doesn't say that either. But Pastor Benton could not have done this horrible thing." She slapped her hand on the table. The silverware rattled. "We're talking about murder!"

Earl took his napkin and dabbed at the table where his coffee spilled. "Two men went into that room. Only one of them came back out alive. A lobby full of people watched the whole thing. How many people do you think were standing there . . . fifty? Sixty?"

"Probably more than that, but —"

"Then," Earl continued, "he comes out in a hurry to leave. The sheriff finds the murder weapon *in his pocket.*"

Gloria's voice trembled. "I'm sure there's an explanation. Maybe that wasn't the murder weapon."

Earl grunted. "So, your theory is that he was carrying a completely different blood-soaked letter opener?"

"Don't take that tone with me, Earl Walker!"

The waitress returned. "What'd y'all decide?"

Earl, Gloria, and Jenny stared at each other. None of them had looked at the menu since the waitress last visited.

"Just something simple," Gloria mumbled. "What pies do you have?"

The waitress wrinkled her nose. "Just what's on the menu."

"Oh. Um . . ." Gloria scanned the back of the menu, adjusting her glasses. Finally the waitress impatiently tapped on the menu with her pen. Gloria said, "Okay . . . I'll have a slice of the banana cream pie."

Earl handed over the menu. "Same for me."

"Fine, two pies." She looked at Jenny. "And you, ma'am?"

Jenny asked, "What's the fish of the day?"

The waitress seemed annoyed. "We're out of fish."

Jenny blinked. "But it's the fish of the day."

The waitress waved to indicate the packed dining room. "You see all these folks here? They ordered the fish of the day."

"Fine. I'll have the banana cream pie."

The waitress scribbled their orders down. "I don't know what's going on down the road, but you'd think the president was shot or something."

"We know," Earl said. "We were there."

The waitress grinned, her eyes flickering to all three at the table. "Really? What happened out there?"

Gloria pulled her hands close to her chest.

Jenny shook her head. "We're still trying to figure that out ourselves."

The waitress leaned on the table. It wobbled. "I heard there was a murder of some sort."

Earl dabbed at the spilled coffee. "We heard that, too."

"But you didn't see it?"

"No. We didn't actually *see* it."

The waitress stood sharply, making the table shake again. "Well, I never! You folks shouldn't go around telling people you know a thing."

As she stormed off, Earl shook his head.

He wanted to chuckle but didn't have it in him.

Jenny said, "What I don't understand is what the pastor said to us. You know, that Montague Black wasn't even in the room. I mean, everyone saw him go in there, right?"

Earl nodded. "That bothered me, too. If you go into a room and you kill the other guy, why not try some kind of self-defense plea?"

Gloria narrowed her eyes. "What do you mean?"

"Nobody knows what happened in that room, except for two people — and one of them is now dead. You could tell any story and at least try to make a jury believe it."

"But what if it's more than just the two people?" Gloria crumpled up her napkin and wiped her nose. "Do we know who else might have been in that room?"

Earl said, "Well, Pastor Benton said that nobody was in there. Since there was a dead body in the room, he was off by at least one person. That's weird enough without figuring that he was off by more than one." Earl looked down at his coffee. "It's not like a bunch of people were planning to jump out and yell 'surprise' or anything."

Gloria sighed. "What could it mean?"

Earl sat back, thinking. Gloria sat back,

thinking. Jenny sat back, thinking.

Earl, stroking his chin, sat forward. "Well . . ." As he paused, the ladies leaned forward. He continued. "The psychic in question, Montague Black, has apparently exhibited some amazing powers. That is, if you can believe the press."

Gloria huffed. "Ugh! The press!"

Earl waved his hand. "I'm just saying, if he really did have some special abilities . . . what if he somehow disappeared out of that room?"

Jenny tilted her head. "And then re-appeared as a" — her voice dropped to a whisper — "a corpse?"

The waitress arrived with a tray. She dropped each plate on the table with a rattle, turned abruptly, and left.

Earl once again dabbed the coffee that spilled on the table. That waitress was not going to get a good tip. "You know, The Shadow had the power to cloud men's minds."

Jenny wrinkled her nose. "Who?"

"Before your time. *The Shadow* was an old-time radio drama."

"And what did he do?"

"Well, I was just saying that he had this sort of hypnotic power that allowed him to be in a room with the gangsters or the criminals or whoever, and they couldn't see him. He was just this *disembodied* voice."

Jenny nibbled on her lower lip. "Are you saying Montague Black was actually in the room, but Pastor Benton couldn't see him?"

Earl shook his head. "No." He pushed away his plate of pie. He wasn't hungry.

Gloria wiped her nose again. "Maybe if Black hypnotized Pastor . . ."

"I can't believe that." Earl locked his fingers together thoughtfully. "There seems to be two possibilities: Pastor Benton is telling the truth — in which case, the psychic was not in that room. Or Pastor Benton is lying — and the psychic was in that room, and the pastor murdered him while dozens of people waited outside." Earl sat back in his wheelchair. "Frankly, I don't know which option is harder to believe."

Nobody touched their pie. Gloria asked, "So, what are you going to do about it?"

Chapter Six

Earl stared out the passenger window as Gloria drove back to Heritage Care. "I'm still not sure why it all comes down to me."

Jenny, in back, put her hands on Earl's headrest. "How can you say that, Mr. Walker?"

Earl turned but couldn't quite see her. The angle made his neck hurt, so he turned back to the windshield. "It's pretty easy to say, College. We're just a bunch of amateurs. We should let the professionals handle it. They're trained for this sort of thing." He grunted. "You saw them all there . . . the sheriff, the deputy —"

Gloria let out a loud harrumph. Earl flashed a smile at her then continued. "— the doctor, the EMTs, all those other people. We're not going to find anything of importance that they couldn't."

Jenny let out a big huff. "How can you say that? You did already."

"What are you talking about?"

"*You* were the one who knew that George Kent was murdered. *You* were the one who figured out what happened."

Gloria added, "If you hadn't gotten involved, the killer would've gotten away with it."

"That was different. The police didn't even know a murder had been committed." Earl stared out the windshield. For long moments, all he could hear was the sound of the car engine. "Here, the police are certainly on top of it. And, as much as it hurts to say it, they already have their man."

Gloria snapped, "How can you say that?"

"Pastor Benton was the only person in or out of that room at the time of the murder. He had the murder weapon in his pocket. It's . . ." Earl felt himself choking up. "It's impossible for him *not* to have committed it."

Jenny challenged him. "Then why are we going back?"

"Don't ask me. This was your idea."

Nobody spoke again until they reached Heritage Care. Gloria had no trouble parking close to the front.

Jenny got the wheelchair out of the trunk, and both ladies helped Earl into it. The three of them reached the entrance and got in with no problem.

"You'd think the place would be locked up tight," Earl said.

A voice shot across the lobby. "The residents here still need all the access they can get — being old and feeble and all." Deputy Fisher crossed the lobby. "We had another deputy posted, but I came to relieve him." He tipped his hat to the ladies. "Ma'am. Jenny." He looked at Earl with a mildly annoyed expression. "So, what are you folks doing back here?"

Earl met his gaze, sure the deputy already knew the answer. He said, "We were just at the diner, talking over events."

"I'm sure."

"We find it difficult to believe Pastor Benton could commit a cold-blooded murder."

The deputy's manner softened. "I have a hard time believing it myself." He pushed back his hat. "I mean, what if we missed something?"

Jenny straightened her back. "That's why we're here. Maybe Mr. Walker here will see something you didn't."

"I can't let you look at a crime scene. You might corrupt it."

"But Mr. Walker solved that other —"

The deputy set his mouth in a grim line.

"Now, listen. That happened one time. The sheriff's office handles calls every day. We deal with crimes. Every day. We maintain the peace. Every day." He rubbed his eyes and let out a big sigh. "Folks, I understand your feelings. I really do." He took off his hat and looked at Jenny. "I wish things were different, but they're not. Things are the way they are."

Gloria sniffled. Jenny folded her arms. Earl stared at the door barred by the yellow tape.

The deputy continued. "I like the pastor, too. But he was the only one in the room. He had the murder weapon in his pocket. It is impossible for him not to be the killer." He held out his hands and shrugged. "There's no other way to look at it."

Earl grunted. "If your case is so airtight, why is the room all closed up?"

"We have to keep everyone out until the crime scene can be cleaned. Besides, you don't know the kooks who want to come to a crime scene." He looked at Gloria and Jenny. "Present company excepted, of course."

"Then," Earl pressed, "there's no harm in us just taking a look? If you already have your case?"

Deputy Fisher furrowed his brow. Then

he relented. "Fine. Just don't touch anything."

Getting into the room meant pulling back the yellow tape and simply opening the door. The deputy stepped aside and motioned for the others to enter then followed them inside. "So, this is where Montague Black was stabbed. Those glass doors were closed and locked. The only way in or out," he said as he turned and pointed, "was through that door to the lobby."

Earl pushed forward the rims of his wheels, scanning the room with his eyes. It seemed to be a sitting room. To his right was a fireplace. To his left were a couple of comfortable chairs and a couch, which looked quite plush. Small end tables sat on either side of the couch. A rolltop writing desk was pressed against the far wall.

Wheeling toward the big glass windows, Earl took note of the carpet. It was a bright red, with ornate patterns formed by gold and black lines of varying widths crisscrossing. There was some spider pattern. "Something spilled here?"

"That's blood."

"Oh."

The far wall was made of a series of glass panels reaching from floor to ceiling. Around the middle of the glass wall was a set of sliding glass doors.

Earl swiveled around to look back the way he'd come. Now, with the glass doors behind him, the fireplace was on his left, the couch and furniture on his right. From this angle, the wallpaper really stood out. It seemed to have a pink hue, thin stripes of black and red alternating every few inches. On the wall to his right, over the writing desk, hung a framed painting of a ship — a whaling vessel? — sailing against a storm.

The wall now facing him was blank but for the wallpaper. But there was something. . . .

Earl pushed forward a few feet, squinting. No, it was just an empty wall.

Deputy Fisher continued his monologue. "Based on all the eyewitness accounts, there were never more than two people in this room at any one time — before, during, or after the time of the murder."

"Stop calling it that," Gloria said, voice quivering. "It could have been self-defense."

The deputy gave her pitying look. "The pastor hasn't claimed that. He keeps telling that crazy story. . . ."

Earl snapped his eyes to the deputy. "What'd he say?"

"He claims the room was empty. That Black wasn't in here. Which would have to mean that, after the pastor left the room, Black magically *rematerialized* as a corpse." He snorted. "That's not going to go over well with the jury."

Earl scratched the side of his nose. "Is there some way Black could have been hiding in here?"

Deputy Fisher, chewing on his lip, strode around the room. He looked at the striped wallpaper walls, at the wall of glass panels, at the fireplace. "Nothing in here is big enough to hide inside. I mean, maybe behind the couch, but I think you'd see their feet underneath. Besides, the body wasn't behind the couch."

Jenny asked, "What if it was some kind of illusion? Maybe he was hiding somewhere in plain sight?"

The deputy shook his head. "Either way, he certainly didn't stab himself."

"One problem at a time." Earl pushed himself toward the fireplace. There was a lot of blackness on the inside, but it had clearly been cleaned out. There were no ashes, no fragments of wood, nothing left inside the grate.

He turned to the others. "What about the fireplace? Could someone have climbed up the chimney?"

The deputy got close and stooped to look

up. He flinched and jumped back, brushing off his brown uniform shirt. "I don't think so, Mr. Walker. Besides, neither the victim nor the" — he shot a glance at Jenny — "suspect had any kind of soot on their person."

"But what if someone climbed down from the outside?"

The deputy looked on the carpet. "That would have left footprints."

"Well, does it slide out? Maybe a secret door?"

Fisher stared at the fireplace dumbly.

Jenny let out a disgusted sigh and lurched at it. "Here, let me check." She began pressing against the mantel, against the bricks, against —

"Hey!" Deputy Fisher pointed. "You're not supposed to touch anything."

Jenny held out her hand. "Do you have a handkerchief?"

The deputy stared a second, then he pulled a white cloth from his back pocket. Wrapping it around her hand, Jenny resumed her search. She tried each brick, several spots on the mantel, the brackets on the mantel, the brackets on the grate, even pulled on each of the fireplace tools.

After some minutes, Earl doubted she'd find any secret switches or compartments.

"I think that's enough, College."

She stopped, her eyes lighting up. "Wait a second!" The other three waited for her to elaborate. She added, "We read a story in one of my literature classes where this guy was shot in a locked room, and the murderer somehow escaped without leaving any evidence how he got out or where he went."

Gloria wrung her hands. The deputy put his hands on his hips.

Earl raised an eyebrow. "And . . . ?"

"The solution was that he shoved a mirror up the chimney."

Earl grunted. "That was the solution? How did that do anything? You have to connect those dots for me."

"Well, it's a thing that happened in the story. It's too complicated to explain — you'll have to read the book." She turned to the fireplace and, using the deputy's handkerchief, carefully opened the grate. Getting on her knees, she twisted and looked up the chimney. "I don't see anything." Her voice echoed in the confined space.

She reached up and felt around. Some soot fell, but that was it. She stood back up, wiping her face with the rag. Both were black now. "Nothing."

Earl snorted. We're not gonna find the answer in some book, College."

Gloria said, "Bless your heart."

The deputy reluctantly accepted his black cloth back, stuffing it back in his pocket. Then he looked at Earl. "What about a secret panel?"

Jenny pointed weakly at the fireplace. "But I just —"

"No," the deputy said. "I meant in the walls — you know, secret panels, hidden doors, trick windows? Isn't that how the magicians do it?"

For the next several minutes, Earl watched the others tap the walls, rapping their knuckles over a few inches at a time, listening for any differences in the tenor of the *rap, rap, rap.* Gloria turned her attention to the floor. She began stomping, once, twice, then moving to another spot and doing it again: *stomp, stomp.* No part of the floor caught her suspicion.

Jenny looked up. "What about the ceiling?"

The deputy said, "It's too high for a person to get up there without a ladder or something. Besides, it's solid white plaster."

"What's this here?" Jenny was at the set of glass doors. "It looks like a handprint. Is this blood?"

The deputy scrutinized it. "Yeah, the crime scene techs tested that. It's the victim's handprint."

Earl asked, "And the blood?"

The deputy nodded. "Yes, the blood was also the victim's."

Earl sighed. "Well, that's something."

The deputy said, "It sure makes it look bad for your pastor. This pretty much proves the man was murdered!"

Earl grunted. "Not necessarily by the pastor. If that had been the pastor's handprint, it would have proven he *had* come in contact with the body after it was stabbed."

The deputy frowned. "What's the difference?"

"It means the pastor's story may sound crazy, but it hasn't been disproven." Earl motioned toward the door. "Maybe the killer came in from out there."

"When the body was found, the doors were closed and locked from the inside." The deputy pushed back his hat. "As much as I would love for us to find something to clear the pastor, I gotta tell ya . . . it looks hopeless."

Earl nodded grimly. Gloria was biting her trembling lip, close to tears. Jenny collapsed onto one of the chairs.

Deputy Fisher took off his hat, fiddling with it in his hands. "You're going to have to face facts. We professionals know what we're doing."

A loud harrumph came from Gloria's direction.

The deputy looked up. "What's that supposed to mean?"

"You locked me up." Gloria pointed a shaky finger.

"Maybe, but we also let you go."

Earl's face felt warm. He wanted to jump to Gloria's defense but wasn't sure how.

Jenny stood, putting fists on her hips. "Landon Fisher, you don't pick on a nice lady like Mrs. Logan. It's not her fault if you people get crazy and lock up the first person —"

Fisher whined, "Hold on, that's not fair! You were there. You know what happened!" He sheepishly pointed in Earl's general direction. "Besides, it was Mr. Walker who actually got Mrs. Logan arrested —"

Earl grunted. "Don't bring me into this!"

Deputy Fisher averted his eyes. Through clenched teeth, he said, "If I was picking on you, Mrs. Logan, I apologize." He put on his hat and began pacing the big room. "The fact remains, Sheriff Meyer had all kinds of professional people here. Law enforcement professionals. The coroner. A crime scene photographer. Crime scene technicians. Medical personnel." He looked at Jenny. “I don’t know what a psychology student and a couple of retirees expect to find, but we don’t need your help.”

Earl pointed to the glass doors. “Tell me about the garden outside.”

Chapter Seven

The deputy used the blackened handkerchief to unlock and open the sliding glass door. He led the others outside. "I don't know what y'all expect to find. The body was here, and the door was locked from the inside."

"When a magician disappears into thin air," Earl said, "there has to be a logical answer. Those guys can fake all kinds of things. There may be some trick to lock the door from outside, and then exit out this way."

"But — again — the body was inside the room. Besides, Black was not actually a magician," Deputy Fisher said. "He claimed to be something called a 'channelist.' You know, a psychic — reads minds, tells the future, stuff like that."

Earl pointed back at the door behind them. "If he disappeared from that room, he was a magician."

"We only have the word of the suspect. Faced with a murder conviction, a man can say all kinds of crazy things."

Gloria blurted, "But isn't that the thing? If the pastor was really guilty, he'd come up with a better explanation than that."

"Well . . ."

Earl squinted one eye at the deputy. "In all your years, have you ever been confronted by a worse alibi?"

The other man pondered a second. "No. Can't say I ever have."

Earl pushed himself farther out on the stone patio. "All the more reason to think there's something fishy about all this."

"Hold on a second," the deputy said. "Look, I hate to believe Pastor Benton murdered that man in cold blood. But that's easier to believe than the idea that Montague Black killed himself to prove some kind of point."

Earl didn't answer. He took stock of the backyard of the facility. It was an old building with high walls. The garden was large and elaborate. Earl could see two exits from the house into the garden. But there was no exit from the garden into the world outside; all around it ran a tall hedge.

"So, Black entered the room before Pastor Benton. Maybe he came out here to hide, you know, pull one of his little psychic stunts. Maybe he came out for a cigarette, or for some fresh air . . . and he wandered out of sight." Earl swiveled around to face the others. "So the pastor comes into the room, he doesn't see anybody in there, he waits for a while, then he finally gets frustrated and storms out."

The deputy seemed bewildered. "And how does the corpse fit in?"

Earl shook his head. "Maybe he was murdered out here and dragged inside. Maybe he was with somebody, and the second man killed him."

"Nope, nope, nope." The deputy ticked a list off with his fingers: "The glass doors were closed and locked — from the inside. The body was right out in plain sight. And when the pastor came out of the room, he had the murder weapon in his pocket." The deputy looked at Earl. "Explain that!"

Jenny blurted, "You don't have to be so smug!"

The deputy looked hurt. "How am I being smug? You people are only in here because I let you. You don't even belong here — you're a bunch of nosy outsiders! I'm the one with the law on my side, with the evidence on my side, with science . . . If I'm being smug, it's only because I have a right to be." He shifted his weight. "But I'm not being smug."

Earl grunted. "You don't know it's the murder weapon. The tests can't be finished yet."

"Fine. Suspected murder weapon. Whatever."

"Not 'whatever.' You should say what you mean."

"Fine." The deputy walked away.

Earl wheeled himself down the sidewalk, deeper into the garden. His wheels caught on some rock or stone in the path. He stopped, backed up a few inches, and went around the small item in his way. The entire place seemed to be enclosed, the tall trees throwing enormous shadows everywhere. Something about it made him think of the Garden of Eden. Everything was pure and innocent — until sin entered the picture, and then it was all taken away.

"So, that's it," the deputy said. "No practical way in or out of this garden, except through those two doors. And the doors into the media room were blocked by a large table."

Earl wheeled himself around. "But if we're talking about some kind of escape artist . . ." He looked up at the high windows and pointed tentatively. "I wonder . . ."

Fisher looked up, taking off his hat to shield his eyes from the sun. He glanced at Earl then back up at the high windows. "You think some kinda human spider crawled up that wall?"

"Hmm. I guess not."

Jenny cried out, "What about these?" The others found her kneeling, looking closely at something in the thick grass.

Deputy Fisher knelt down next to her. "Whatcha got?"

"Cigarette butts."

"Eh." The deputy stood back up. "Those could have been left at any time."

Earl grunted. "Are they wet?"

Jenny found the courage to pick one up. "I don't think so." She handed it to the deputy, who nodded in agreement.

Gloria asked, "What does it mean?"

Earl said, "It means they could have been dropped here sometime today."

The deputy shook his head. "That's stretching it a bit, don't you think?"

"I said 'could.' "

A voice crackled from inside the thick trees. "Who's out here?" An elderly black man appeared, brandishing a rake.

Deputy Fisher put on his hat, puffed out his chest, and straightened to his full height. "I'm Deputy Landon Fisher of the Fletcher

County Sheriff's Department. And who might you be?"

The man lowered his rake. "Sorry, Deputy. I'm Ebenezer Wilson. I'm in charge of the grounds."

Earl said, "Hello, Mr. Wilson. I'm Earl Walker, this is Mrs. Gloria Logan, and this is Miss Jenny Hutton." The other man nodded his head politely.

The deputy added, "They're, uh, special investigators, here under my, er, protection."

"Uh-huh."

"So, what do you do around here?"

The man looked confused. "I take care of the grounds."

"I know," Fisher said. "But what all does that mean?"

The man waved his rake around him. "Well, we got our trees over here, we got the grass over there, the shrubs along there. I trim what needs trimmin', I pull up the weeds —"

"Fine, fine." The deputy waved his hands. "What I meant was . . ." He leaned toward Earl and murmured, "What did I mean?"

Earl turned to Wilson and smiled. "Were you here during the, uh . . . excitement?"

"Yep." The man nodded. "I was out along the back yanking on the weeds. And then someone locked me out here."

Deputy Fisher and Earl exchanged a look. Then they looked at the man. Fisher asked, "You say somebody locked you out here?"

The man nodded. "Yep. I was out working along the back there —"

The deputy cut him off. "Then what'd you do?"

"What do you mean?"

"When you found out you'd been locked out, what'd you do? Where'd you go?"

"Well, I guess I had a smoke and then worked on the weeds."

Jenny pointed to the cigarette butts in the grass. "So, these are yours?"

Mr. Wilson peered. "Yes, I imagine those are."

Earl frowned. "But if you're responsible for the grounds, why would you —"

"I was going to pick them up later. I was just what you call *stressed* at the time. I was working out here in the sun, and then I finished up my water jug. I came up to get some more and found the sliding doors locked tight. Of course, I have a set of keys, so I didn't think a whole lot about it." The man picked up his rake. "What's this all about, if I may ask?"

The deputy cleared his throat. "Well, I'm sorry to tell you that a man was murdered this morning."

Mr. Wilson's face fell. "Here?"

"Yes sir. It seems to have taken place in the sitting room."

"Oh." The man started to wobble then supported himself on the rickety fence. "And do you know who did it?"

"Well, we have a suspect in custody . . . but we're still conducting an investigation."

The deputy squinted. "How many ways can a person get out of this garden?"

"This whole area back here is fenced all around. This place is completely closed in." With his hand, he indicated the circumference around them. "Building's on this side, and fences and shrubs go all the way around. You can only leave the garden that way." He pointed back toward the building and pulled a red kerchief out of his back pocket and wiped his forehead. "We got a lot of old folks living here. Wouldn't want any of them to wander off and get hurt."

Earl rubbed his chin. "So a person could have been hiding behind that couch in there, jumped Black and killed him, then run out here. But anyone who came out here would be trapped."

Jenny started, "Maybe someone came in from the outside —"

The deputy shook his head. "No. If there's no way out, there's no way in."

"Maybe a helicopter —"

"Seriously?" The deputy waved his arms. "Look, I like the pastor as much as y'all, but do you really want me to tell the sheriff that somebody dropped in here by parachute and then killed our victim and then ran out here and then, I don't know, somehow *ninja'ed* their way out of the garden and got away?"

Earl looked at the shrubs lining the edge of the garden. They seemed too tall for a man to jump over. "How thick are those? Can someone climb those bushes or push his way through?"

Mr. Wilson shook his head. "Nope. Too thick to go through, too prickly to climb over."

The deputy said, "How about climbing over the fence?"

"Nope."

Earl asked, "How well do you know the building?"

"W–what do you mean?"

"You say there's only one way in or out of the garden, right? What about inside the house? If a person is in that room and the doors are closed and locked from the inside, is there some other way out?"

The old man shook his head, his eyes glassy. "I don't follow you."

"Perhaps a secret door? Maybe some kind of secret passage?"

The man seemed indignant. "What kind of place do you think this is?"

"I didn't mean any disrespect, sir. It just seems kind of unsafe to be back here and completely locked out. What if there's a fire or something — surely there's some emergency exit?"

"Well, we do have the other door. But we're —"

"You mean where they set up the media room?"

"No, sir. There's another entrance over —"

The deputy snapped his head. "You said there was no other door!"

"We're renovating that part of the house. It's completely blocked off."

"Show me."

The old man collected himself, stood, wiped his face with his red cloth, and led them across the grass back to the path. The deputy was hot on the man's heels, so Gloria and Jenny had to help Earl wheel across the grass.

Earl saw something. "Wait. Stop."

Gloria asked, "What's the matter?"

"I think it's a wrapper." Earl stretched for it.

Jenny bent down and got it for him. "Do you think it's important?"

"Could be." He pocketed it.

Finally, they caught up with the two men standing at the far left of the building. Piled around were bags of cement, wooden planks, and bricks, all covered with a clear plastic tarp. Earl's eyes went to the boarded-up space in the brick wall. Anyone who came in or out that way — even if one could do so — would have to climb over the collection of junk. And there was no way to do so without walking on the loose dirt and leaving footprints.

"Mr. Wilson," Deputy Fisher asked, "when you heard this so-called *'ruckus,'* did you hear anything unusual? Or see anything unusual?"

"I'm not sure what you mean."

"You know, weird voices, ghostly apparitions, anything just bizarre."

Earl and Gloria exchanged a confused glance.

The old man seemed to give it some thought. "Um . . . Nope."

The deputy seemed satisfied. "Thank you, sir. We won't trouble you any more." He led the others back inside.

"Well," Earl grumbled, "Black didn't go out into the garden."

Fisher took off his hat and lowered his eyes. "I'm sorry, folks. Genuinely sorry. But you just can't fight the facts." He checked his watch. "The other deputy will be back to take his post."

Earl, Gloria, and Jenny filed out to the lobby without a word. They made their way to the exit.

At the exit, Deputy Fisher called Jenny aside. They conversed in low tones and then hugged. The deputy saw Earl watching, blushed, and went back inside.

Gloria asked Earl, "What now?"

He locked his fingers together. "We still have the same two options: Either the pastor is telling the truth, or the pastor is lying. And if he's telling the truth, then that psychic man was not in the room. But there's no physical explanation for it."

Gloria's cell phone rang. She checked it. "It's the prayer chain again." She answered and spoke for a few minutes. When she got off, she was ashen.

Earl asked, "What is it?"

"The church elders want to replace Pastor Benton."

Chapter Eight

None of them had much to say in the car. Earl felt like the wind had been knocked out of him. It was bad enough for him to have doubts about Pastor Benton's innocence, but for the man's own church to be ready to kick him to the curb before he even had his say in front of a jury . . .

Earl glanced at Jenny, who was sulking in the backseat. He turned to Gloria, behind the wheel. "So, what'd they say?"

Gloria sniffled as she started the car. "They want to hold an emergency vote."

"Tomorrow morning? In church?"

"No, Friday night. They're going to call it a business meeting."

As he gazed vacantly out the car window, vaguely aware of the sun warming his face, Earl wondered what he was doing. The events of the morning and afternoon had happened so quickly that he had been swept away without getting the chance to process it.

What did he really think happened at the nursing home that morning? What did he really expect to find at the scene of the crime? Maybe the deputy was right — he needed to let the professionals handle this.

Celebrity psychic Montague Black and Pastor Andrew Benton both walked into that room alive. A lobby packed with witnesses attested to that. The sliding door was locked from the inside; the only possible exit was back into the crowded lobby outside the door.

Of those two men, only Pastor Benton came out alive. He didn't say, "Black dropped dead" or "Black attacked me, and I had to kill him in self-defense." He claimed Black wasn't there at all — yet the body was found sprawled on the floor in plain sight. And the pastor tried to get away with the murder weapon in his pocket.

Riding in the car, listening to the hum of the road, Earl had a chance to think. No longer swept up in the adrenaline rush to solve the puzzle, he could finally sort through the information jammed into his head. Figure out what he really thought. How he really felt.

Earl thought about everything he owed to

Pastor Benton. When Earl had lost his home after the Candlewick scandal, it was the pastor and his family who took him in. They had given him a place to stay for the interim, had given him his dignity. They had shown Earl the love of Jesus in a way that was practical and real, not like the stuff he'd seen on TV.

The memories flooded over Earl. Pastor Benton at church with his congregation. Pastor Benton at home with his family. Pastor Benton in the office counseling Earl.

When Earl was down, the pastor gave him the benefit of the doubt. Earl decided he was not about to deny Pastor Benton the same in return.

Gloria reached the turnoff for Earl's apartment complex. She pulled into the parking lot and switched off the ignition. Her hands dropped to her sides. In the backseat behind her, Jenny sat like a rock.

Earl said, "We need to talk to some people — staff, onlookers, the man's entourage . . ."

Gloria looked at him. "For what?"

Jenny leaned forward. "What are you doing?"

"We need to figure out who was there at the time of the murder — who, in addition to Pastor Benton, also had the opportunity, who had the means."

Gloria asked, "But what about this meeting at church?"

"What about it?"

"They don't want to even wait and see how the trial turns out."

"When did you say it was?"

"Friday night. Although I'm sure they'll be talking about it tomorrow morning at —"

"Look," Earl said, "the best thing we can do between now and then is prove Pastor Benton is innocent. Don'tcha think?"

That night, Earl made a list of suspects. The names on the short list were: (1) Sheree Jackson at Heritage Care; (2) Hamilton Page, the man writing the true-crime book; (3) Divina Zuniga, the TV producer woman who'd apparently created some kind of Montague Black show; and (4) Jack Carpenter, the man's manager. As he had listed off the names to Jenny, Earl did not explain to the ladies why he considered each of them to be a suspect. That is, he hadn't explained to them entirely.

Not to mention the other eighty or ninety folks also packed into the lobby . . .

The next morning, Earl couldn't bring himself to go to church. The thought of all those holier-than-thou Holy Rollers looking down their noses and yelling at each other was more than Earl could stomach.

He also failed to call and tell Gloria he wasn't going. When she arrived at his door and found him still in his robe and pajamas, she was not thrilled. But she didn't push it.

They made plans to meet the next day. She'd take a personal day off work. Jenny would skip her classes at school.

And Gloria stressed that Earl better be dressed in street clothes for that.

Monday morning, Earl was indeed dressed for his guests. Jenny arrived first. At Earl's insistence, she fixed herself some eggs and toast and poured herself some juice. While she was at it, he said, he wouldn't mind having some himself.

Gloria arrived second. She had already eaten breakfast but took the toast Earl offered her, to be sociable. When Jenny got back to the table and saw that Earl had given her toast away, she went back to the kitchen to make some more.

"I saw that the church made the news." Earl found he had to avert his eyes. "So how did it go yesterday? I'm almost afraid to ask."

"One of the deacons did the sermon."

Gloria let out a big sigh. "Afterward, there was a lot of bluster from some members about the situation with Pastor Benton."

"Why? What business is it of theirs?"

She pasted some purple jam on her slice of toast. "Well, technically, it's the business of every member of church. It would be your business, too, if you'd finish your new-members' class."

"I only missed the one time."

"You missed twice."

"That other time I wasn't feeling well."

"You felt well enough to watch wrestling."

"I've told you, it's perfectly acceptable for sick people to watch television while they recuperate." He saw Jenny coming back from the kitchen with her toast. "Isn't it?"

"I'm not taking sides again."

"Fine." He turned back to Gloria. "So these people are blustering because . . . ?"

"Some members think the fact that Pastor Benton is even associated with a murder is reason enough to dismiss him."

"But he hasn't been convicted!" He turned to Jenny again, finally buttering her own toast. He said, "Were you at church?"

"Yes. Everyone was there." She shrugged. "Well, except —"

"All right, all right. So these people were blustering. . . ."

Gloria nodded. "They don't seem to care whether Pastor Benton is cleared or not. It isn't a question of guilt; it's a question of association. They don't like the name of the church being 'dragged through the gutter.' "

Jenny added, "A bunch of the media was there, too."

"Yes," Gloria agreed. "Which only made the, um, loud members even more certain of their cause."

"So, they were all ready to vote the poor man out, huh?" Earl shook his head. "I just can't believe it."

"No," Jenny said, chewing her eggs. She swallowed. "It felt like most of them want to wait until this business is resolved." Her eyes dropped. "But there could be a motion to begin a search for candidates for a new pastor — just in case."

"Hey, I need to show you something." Earl wheeled for the living room. He grabbed his Bible off the coffee table and returned, plopping it on the table. He flipped to a place he had marked. "Listen to this: In the book of Exodus, starting in chapter seven, Moses faced off with the court magicians in Egypt." He looked up. "With the power of God, Moses was demonstrating all these amazing things. Did you know he had a staff that could turn into a snake?"

Gloria smiled. "Uh-huh."

Earl continued. "And the Pharaoh's court magicians were able to counterfeit these powers . . . to a point. But then there came that point where Moses was calling down these plagues in the name of God, and the magicians were just left in the dust . . . so to speak." When Gloria and Jenny stared, he added, "I found it in my lesson book from the new-members' class."

Gloria and Jenny exchanged a look. Then they both looked at Earl. He looked back. "I didn't just watch wrestling yesterday, you know."

Jenny had gone on the Internet and printed out directions to the offices of celebrated psychic and murder victim Montague Black. The three hoped that was where they'd find the man's manager, Jack Carpenter. They didn't have any reasonable excuse to expect him to talk to them, but Earl had to try.

Reaching the office building, they were in the parking garage when they met up with Deputy Landon Fisher. He seemed less puzzled than annoyed to see them. "Now what are you folks doing here?"

Jenny curled some strands of blond hair behind her ear. "We were just, um . . ."

The big man let out a sigh, nodding. "I

know why you're here. I just — why *are* you here?"

Earl squinted at him. "Huh?"

"I thought we went through this the other day. You folks aren't supposed to be meddling in an investigation."

Earl cocked an eyebrow. "But there is no investigation. You already arrested your man, didn't you?"

The deputy's bluster was piddling out. "But that's no excuse to interfere with professional . . ." He let out a big breath. "Look, I still have my doubts, too. But the sheriff is satisfied, the crime scene techs are satisfied, the district attorney is satisfied. . . ." He held out his arms. "Why aren't *you* satisfied?"

Earl set his jaw. "Why aren't *you?*"

The deputy's arms dropped to his sides. He inhaled deeply and let it out through his nose. The parking garage echoed around them. "It's just . . . something you said."

Earl's eyes widened. "Me?"

"It's how this Montague character seemed to have strange powers. I mean, he told us stuff before we knew it ourselves!" The deputy stepped closer and dropped his voice. "What if he did disappear from the room? Just because we couldn't figure out a way to do it doesn't mean he didn't. Maybe he opened some demonic portal. . . ."

"What did Black's manager say about all this? I assume you just spoke with him."

Deputy Fisher removed his hat, his eyes on it in his hands. "Now, that would be privileged information in the course of an investigation." He looked at Jenny a second then put the hat back on and straightened the brim. "Please do not harass the man. If we get any complaints, we may have to take action against you folks. I would hate to do that."

His walkie-talkie sputtered. A voice barked, "Fisher? Where are you?"

Deputy Fisher's face reddened, and he snatched the walkie-talkie off his belt. "Right here, Sheriff. I'm at the office of Jack Carpenter. What do you need?"

"Carpenter, Carpenter . . . you mean that manager fella? What are you doin' out there? That case is closed!"

Deputy Fisher turned away from the others. He said into his mic, "Well, I was just —"

"You better head on down to the ol' Watson place. Their cow is down in the ditch again."

"Again?" Deputy Fisher turned even farther away from the others. He spoke into the walkie-talkie in a lower voice. "But I've already gotten that cow out twice. Can't she pen it up?"

The voice out of the walkie-talkie boomed, "Now, Landy, you know Mrs. Watson is just a poor old woman. She needs our help. That is, she needs *your* help."

The deputy sighed. "But can't one of the other —"

"Get out there now! Don't make me tell you again!"

Deputy Fisher's shoulders fell. He hesitated. Then he spoke again into the mic. "Yes, Sheriff. Right away." He set the walkie-talkie back on his belt. He turned back and had some trouble making eye contact with the others. He started to say something then just walked off.

After the deputy was gone, Gloria put a hand on Earl's shoulder. "What do we do now?"

Earl turned to look up at her. He shrugged. "We go in."

Jack Carpenter's office was packed. Metal-skeleton shelves were crammed with all manner of office supplies — boxes of envelopes, stacks of paper, plastic containers of rubber bands and paper clips, and Scotch tape. Narrow bookshelves were jammed full with hardcover books and oversize paperbacks. The bulletin board had numerous papers pinned on top of each other, all carefully layered. The credenza against the wall held a collection of enormous antique German beer steins.

When they questioned him, Jack Carpenter, former manager to the late Montague Black, was not forthcoming. "I don't understand all this interest," he told Jenny. He paid most of his attention to her. "It's all pretty cut-and-dried."

Earl cleared his throat. "If you could" — Carpenter would barely acknowledge his presence, but Earl pressed on — "just tell us what you saw. What happened from your perspective?"

The man sat on the edge of his desk. "Well, the reverend lured Black to this meeting with the promise of a public apology —"

"Wait." Earl held a hand up. "It was the other way around. Your man invited the pastor."

The man shook his head slowly. "Nope. I distinctly remember the pastor calling us — well, his assistant or somebody — and making arrangements. He said he was embarrassed about how that liturgy of his got released to the media." Carpenter looked at Jenny. "You know, that clip said it all —

what was it? — 'kill all the magicians.' "

" 'Thou shalt not suffer a witch to live,' " she corrected softly. It was barely above a whisper.

"Anyway, it's like the sheriff's office worked out — two men went in; only one came out. There was like a hundred witnesses." He turned to Jenny again. "You were there."

She nodded glumly.

Earl locked his fingers together. "Then what happened?"

"Well, it's a matter of public record — your reverend came out in a hurry and tried to get away. I was worried about Montague and went to check on him. I saw the body lying on the floor. I ran out and yelled that someone needed to stop the reverend." Carpenter held out his hands. "That's all."

Earl eyed him. "Who had a reason to kill Montague Black?"

"Other than some bloodthirsty Bible-thumper?"

Earl glanced at Gloria, who had stiffened at the man's characterization. Earl turned back to Carpenter and simply said, "Yes."

The man seemed to give it some thought. "I can't think of anybody. I'm not saying the man was beloved by all, but it's not healthy to speak ill of the dead." He rapped his knuckles on the desktop. "Especially when speaking with the dead is your business."

"How about the others who were there with him? What was his relationship like with them?"

Carpenter stood. "Look, folks, this is a bad time. My best friend was just murdered in cold blood, and I have to wrap up all the paperwork that was pending before your reverend . . ." His voice choked. "You'll have to leave."

Earl nodded. "We're sorry for your pain. Just one more question."

The man shot him an annoyed look. "What?"

"How did Montague Black do his disappearing trick?"

"What is it with you people? First the deputy, and now you!" Carpenter waved his arms. "Mr. Black was a psychic — he communed with the dead. He did not do magic tricks. That's completely different." He hustled them toward the door. "Now, that's all the time I have. You have to leave."

At the car, Gloria let out a loud, frustrated sigh. "We're no closer than we were before."

Earl looked away and rubbed his chin. "I wonder . . ." He looked at Jenny. "Can you look up some stuff for me on that World Wide Computernet of yours?"

Chapter Nine

Jenny returned from the library, carrying an armload of books. Earl's eyes goggled. "You found that much?"

She unloaded the books on the coffee table. "I couldn't believe all the stuff I found. Look!"

Earl picked up a few titles, squinting at the selections in his hands. *Death from a Top Hat* by Clayton Rawson, *Nine Times Nine* by Anthony Boucher, *Flowers for the Judge* by Margery Allingham . . .

Gloria grabbed some books and read her titles aloud. *"The Big Bow Mystery, The Kennel Murder Case . . ."*

Earl picked some more titles off the table. *"Have His Carcase, And Then There Were None . . ."* He set them back on the table. "What are all these?"

Jenny blinked. "Classic detective novels."

Earl let out a disgusted sigh. "I thought you were doing research."

Jenny pulled the backpack strap off her shoulder and set the bag down. She dropped onto the couch. "I looked for answers to your questions online. I couldn't find anything. But while I was there, I thought I'd at least get some information we could use."

"Yeah, but detective stories?" Earl was flipping through a collection of Father Brown stories. "Pastor Benton is accused of murder, and you're wasting our time with this stuff?"

"Mr. Walker, these are about problem solving. These aren't just mysteries; they're 'locked-room murders' and 'impossible crimes.' "

"What's the difference?"

"They are . . . wait, I printed some stuff out at the library." Jenny looked through her backpack and pulled out some loose sheets. "Here — 'Locked-Room Murders and Impossible Crimes. A crime, often a murder, committed in a way that it seems impossible to have happened, or seems impossible to determine how it was done.' "

Earl looked at Gloria, who shrugged.

Jenny looked up from the sheet, smiled, and looked for her place again. " 'The standard example where the murder victim's found inside a room with only one single door, which is locked from the inside — and it is not suicide. The story form can also include the unbreakable alibi, the least likely suspect, and the sealed site, where the impossibility is derived from the crime scene's pristine condition. This is the detective story or puzzle mystery at its most intellectual — and can only be solved through ratiocination.' "

Earl squinted. " 'Radio-what'?"

Jenny smiled. " 'Ratiocination.' " She looked through her sheets and frowned. "I thought I printed out the definition. But as I recall, it means 'using pure thinking to figure out the problem.' It comes from Edgar Allan Poe, who —"

"Are you sure this is relevant?"

"Think about it! Of those two men, Pastor Benton — who cannot *possibly* be the murderer — was the only one to come out of that room. And the murder weapon was in his pocket. And Black was murdered inside an enclosed room — the exit was locked from the inside. Doesn't that sound impossible to you?"

Earl sighed loudly. "Fine."

Jenny grabbed one of the books Earl had dropped on the coffee table. "Look at this one, *And Then There Were None,* by Agatha Christie. A small group of people are trapped alone on an island, someone is killing them off one by one, and when the police show up, it's impossible to determine who did it."

Earl waved his hands impatiently. "So, what happened? How'd the killer do it?"

"I'm not going to tell you the ending."

"Why not? You were the one who raised the —"

"That's what the *story* is for — you read the story to see how it turns out."

He sighed. "Fine."

"I think I saw that movie," Gloria said helpfully. She wrinkled her nose. "It wasn't my favorite."

"The book is better than the movie," Jenny said. She checked through her printouts again. "I have some examples of stories about impossible crimes."

Earl rubbed his temple. "Go ahead."

Jenny ran her finger along the sheet: "A flatbed train car is stolen out of the middle of a moving train. A man all alone in a phone booth is stabbed in the back with an ice pick. A child disappears from an airplane in the middle of the flight. A man by himself in a room is shot by a bullet fired more than 200 years earlier. A football player is tackled on the field and vanishes from the bottom of the pile. A man whose throat was cut is found on a rock surrounded by wet sand which has no footprints — and the fisherman on a nearby fishing boat swears nobody approached the beach for hours."

Earl squeezed his temple. "And these are all made-up stories?"

Jenny shuffled through her papers. "There are also examples of true crimes that —"

Earl held out a hand. "Let me see."

She handed over the sheet, and Earl skimmed it:

In 1880s Berlin, a man's wife and children were found dead inside a locked cellar. On first inspection, there seemed no way to unlock or manage the door from outside — the door was so tight in the frame that one could not even slip a sheet of paper through the crack. However, an examiner discovered a small hole inside the door and determined the man had bored a hole through the door, looped a strand of horsehair through the hole to lock the door from the outside, and then used wax and paint to cover the hole on the outside. The man claimed he got the idea from a mystery novel.

In 1898, Empress Elisabeth of Austria-Hungary was stabbed while in a crowd. The killer used a needle file, which created such a thin wound, she did not realize she was fatally injured and walked to her cabin, where she collapsed and died. If she had locked her door behind her, it would have created a locked-room mystery.

In San Francisco, a man was found dead in his locked apartment. Police at first suggested the man may have stabbed himself after taking drugs, but no knife was recovered, and no drugs were found in the man's body. The medical examiner was unable to determine a cause of death.

There were several more sheets of such entries. Earl rubbed his eyes. "And you're telling me these are real?"

"The ones in your hand, yes."

"And these cases here that are still unsolved, are they supposed to be ghost stories or something?"

Jenny furrowed her brow. "No. Look, that's why I have all these mystery stories — the fictional ones, that is — because they show us how to solve an impossible crime."

Earl looked over at Gloria, who had been silent through most of the discussion. "What do you think?"

She smiled awkwardly. "I don't know what to think."

"Look, it's very simple." Jenny let out a

frustrated breath. She looked through the stacks of books on the coffee table until she found one particular volume. She held it up. "This novel is *The Three Coffins.* It's by John Dickson Carr. This is considered one of the all-time classics of the genre."

Earl nodded tentatively. "If you say so."

"If I can find the right chapter . . ." She flipped through until she found her place and tapped it with a finger. "Here! Chapter seventeen — the famous 'locked-room lecture.' The author actually outlines all the kinds of locked-room and impossible-crime scenarios." She skimmed a bit. "Okay, there seems to be seven possible explanations. Ah, here, number one: 'It is not murder, but a series of coincidences ending in an accident which looks like murder.' "

"How does that happen?"

She consulted the page. "Well, there could have been some kind of struggle earlier, before the room was locked — and then at a later time the supposed *'victim'* falls and knocks his head or something. When the body is found, everyone assumes the struggle and the death both happened at the same time." She looked up. "Some Sherlock Holmes stories fall into this category."

Earl grunted. "I can't imagine that Montague Black stabbed himself and then put the knife in Pastor Benton's pocket by some accident."

Jenny faltered. "Um, no, I suppose not." She turned back to the book, searching for her place. "Okay, the second one: 'It is murder, but the victim is impelled to kill himself or crash into an accidental death.' " She skimmed. "This one could be caused by frightening the person to death somehow, or using gas or poison to make the victim go berserk and mess up the room before somehow killing himself."

Gloria said, "That sounds just like the first one."

"In this case, someone deliberately causes it to happen."

Earl frowned. "So . . . someone tricked Black into stabbing himself and then also tricked him into dropping the knife in Pastor Benton's pocket?"

"Um . . ."

Earl nodded curtly. "Uh-huh. Next."

"Oh, um, 'It is a murder, by a mechanical device already planted in the room and hidden undetectably in some innocent-looking piece of furniture.' Oh, this is interesting: It could be some kind of trap set by a person who is now long dead." She looked up. "This can be a mechanical trap of some kind, a concealed gun or a hidden needle.

He even says it could be an electrified glove."

Earl caught himself thinking back to the room — the couch, the chairs, the writing desk, even the fireplace. He shook it off. "No glove. Go on."

"Number four: 'It is suicide, which is intended to look like murder.' " She looked up. "This could be done with a weapon made to vanish. Like you stab yourself with an icicle, which melts before the body is found. Or you shoot yourself with a gun rigged to somehow disappear after you die."

"You mean, like I commit suicide —"

Gloria cut him off in a high-pitched voice, begging, "Can we please move on? This is so morbid!"

Jenny consulted the book again. "Number five: 'A murder which derives its problem from illusion and impersonation.' The victim is already dead, but witnesses think he's still alive because the murderer somehow impersonates him."

"Sounds kinda fancy to me."

Jenny waved her hand over the books. "That's why I checked out all the books, so we could see how —"

"Uh-huh." Earl nodded. "Go on."

"Six: 'It is a murder which, although committed by somebody outside the room at the time, nevertheless seems to have been committed by somebody who must have been inside.' "

Earl nodded. "Interesting. Go on."

"Number seven is the reverse of number five — the illusion is that everyone thinks the victim is already dead when he is actually still alive. He's incapacitated in some way or apparently dead, and the murder is not actually committed until after the room is breached by the witnesses."

Earl sat back in his wheelchair. "I appreciate what you're trying to do here, College, but I don't think any of these are applicable to the situation at hand."

"Well, you sort of have to soak them in. Let them roll around in your mind." Jenny waved a hand over all the books on the coffee table. "I'm not saying one of these books will actually explain what happened in there with Pastor Benton when Montague Black died — but if we can just get into this mindset, it could help us think this through and solve our own problem."

Earl considered what she was saying. The way things were going, it wasn't like possible solutions were leaping out from the bushes. Maybe the college girl was on to something.

Not that he was ready to concede yet.

"Maybe."

She consulted the book again. "Okay, and now they go through ways to kill the guy inside the room then go outside and make the room seem like it had been locked from the inside."

Earl grimaced. He took a deep breath and let it out. "All right," he said. "Lay 'em on me."

"Let's see." Jenny adjusted her glasses, checking the book. "The first one is to tamper with the key, which is still in the lock."

Earl raised an eyebrow. "The key is still in the lock?" How old is this book?"

"Um . . ." Jenny checked the copyright. "1935."

"I see."

She turned back to her place in the book. "The second one is to remove the hinges of the door without disturbing lock or bolt. Hey, that's a neat trick."

"I don't think it's applicable." Earl held out his hands. "What's next on the list?"

Jenny adjusted her glasses again. "Okay, the third one you have tampering with the bolt, and the fourth one, tampering with a falling bar or latch." She read a little further. "And the fifth one is that the murderer commits the crime, locks the door, and keeps the key, but the key is assumed to still be inside. He is the first to raise a scare and breaks the door to get in and simply puts the key back in the lock."

Earl grunted. "Again, locks don't work that way anymore."

"Well, it's not so much the specifics we're looking at as the principle of the thing. If we can just get into the mind-set —"

"This is hopeless." Earl breathed in through his nose and let it out. "I was right before. We had no business getting involved."

Chapter Ten

Earl grabbed the remote and pointed it at the TV. He began flipping through the channels.

Gloria sniffled. "So that's it? You're going to sit back and do nothing?"

"I've been doing nothing this whole time!" He waved his hands across the books on the coffee table. "This is not one of those stories from the library! I'm just an old man in a wheelchair."

Jenny said, "But before, you said we could —"

"I lost my head — caught up in the heat of the moment. But now we have a chance to sit and think about what we're doing." He raised a finger. "Name one thing we've done so far that's made any difference."

Jenny's eyes flashed with anger. "How can you —"

Earl held up a hand. "We all believe Pastor Benton is innocent. But we have to face facts — there's nothing we can do about it."

Gloria, face scrunched up, started digging in her purse. "Well, Mr. Walker, I'm not going to take up any more of your time. I'm not going to stick around here waiting for you to do the right thing."

"Gloria, I —"

"I'm not afraid to go out there and make a fool of myself. Not when a man's life is at stake. There were *two* victims in that room on Saturday. It may be too late for us to help one of them, but we can still save the other."

Jenny asked in a pitiful voice, "So where are you going?"

Gloria had to stop and think about it. "I guess I'm going back to that nursing home."

Earl huffed. "But we didn't find anything in that room."

"I'm going to talk to that woman in charge." Gloria nodded. "She must have seen or heard *something.*"

Jenny got up. "I'll go with you."

"Thank you." Gloria, purse strung across her shoulder, launched for the door, Jenny following. Gloria opened the door but stopped at the doorway and turned back to Earl. "We're not going to waste any more of your time, Mr. Walker."

"Wait!" Earl set his jaw, his dentures shifting. He reached down and gripped the rims of his wheels. "I'm going."

Gloria raised her nose. "We wouldn't want to inconvenience you."

Earl wheeled himself to the door. He grumbled, "A little late for that."

There wasn't much discussion in the car on the way back to Heritage Care. After so many trips back and forth, Gloria knew the way.

As the car wound its way through the country roads, Earl found his thoughts turning to the driver. She was pretty mad. How did this change things?

Should it change things?

He cautiously let his eyes wander around the vehicle. It was a Crown Victoria, a big old boat of a car. Not quite as big as the metro bus that Earl drove for many years, but still pretty big. Gloria liked feeling safe in the big car.

Earl smiled to himself. His late wife, Barbara, had been the same way. It was funny to him how many ways the two women were much alike — and how many ways they couldn't be more different.

He could tell Gloria was fuming as she watched the road. She was giving him the silent treatment. All he could hear was the whine of the engine and the country road under the tires.

Earl turned and saw Jenny in back still sulking. He tried to smile. "Listen, College, I'm sorry about what I said about the books and such. I know you were trying."

She didn't reply. He turned back to his window.

At Heritage Care, they were only a little surprised to run into Deputy Fisher in the parking lot. He snapped, "What's *with* you people?"

Jenny snapped back, "We could say the same about you!"

He motioned them back toward their car. "As an officer of the law, I have to ask you folks to —"

His walkie-talkie crackled. "Fisher! Where are you?"

The deputy snatched his walkie-talkie off his belt and turned away. "I'm, uh . . . out on my rounds, Sheriff."

"You're not out at that place again, are you?"

"I was just responding to another . . . um . . ."

"Drop it in the pond, Deputy! These feds are breathin' down my neck like foxes on a chicken. The last thing I need is one of y'all chasin' ghosts!"

The deputy paused. "Yes, sir."

"Ya hear me?"

"Yes, sir."

"Now, we got a call from the old Hanes farm. Go tell Rye Cooter if he's gonna use an electric fence for his cows, he's gotta charge the fence!"

"Yes, sir."

"I can't understand why a man would string a mile of electric fence and not attach it to anything. The man's a moron."

"Yes, sir."

"So, we're done with the ghost stuff. Right?"

"Yes, sir. No more ghost stuff." The sheriff signed off, and Deputy Fisher attached the walkie-talkie back to the mount on his belt. He turned, embarrassed. "The sheriff's got a lot on his mind." He started to say something else, but nothing came out. His eyes were on his shoes. Finally, he closed his mouth and marched away.

Earl felt bad for the kid. But any kind words that came to mind would just make it more awkward. The squad car pulled out and sped away.

Gloria said, "Bless his heart."

Earl smiled to himself. He'd learned that Gloria — like many women from the South — considered "Bless his heart" a euphemism for "What an idiot." As the dust and gravel settled, Earl put his hands to the rims of his wheels and pushed toward the entrance.

Jenny asked, "I wonder what the sheriff meant about the feds?"

Earl pulled the door open. "The FBI is now in on this serial-killer business. I saw it on the news. I guess with celebrated psychic Montague Black out of the way, the locals need any help they can get."

Inside, they found themselves again in the familiar lobby. The door at the far side was no longer taped off. Jenny said, "Where do we find the manager?"

Earl's eyes scanned the big lobby. He pointed to the closer of the two halls, on their right. "Down that way?"

Following the hall, they passed a series of notices hastily taped to the dingy white walls: NEW OFFICE HOURS. EMERGENCY PROCEDURES. CONTACT INFORMATION.

Earl assumed some of the postings were in response to the recent horrific event. But from this angle, he couldn't read the fine print.

Passing a series of closed doors, they came to an intersection of halls. Gloria said, "I wish there was something posted telling us which way to go."

Earl pointed toward the nearest open door. "Let's just ask."

Inside, they found a man at a desk, absorbed with paperwork. Earl waited for him to notice their presence. Finally, he cleared his throat. "Excuse me."

The man looked up from his papers. Earl recognized him as the bald man from Saturday — the one he saw reprimanding Sheree Jackson. At the interruption, the man's face twisted. "What?"

Earl forced a smile. He hoped it looked polite. "We're trying to find the manager."

"Yes. I'm Paul Mason, the manager."

Earl paused. "We were here at the event the other day, and there seemed to be a young lady who —"

"If you're looking for Ms. Jackson, she's no longer employed here."

"Oh. Um . . ."

The other man stared, apparently unwilling to help his guests out with any further information. He clutched a stack of papers in one hand.

Earl held tightly on to his patience. Forcing his voice to remain steady, he asked, "Would you help us to contact her?"

"We are not allowed to give that information out."

Earl was stumped. Finally, he grumbled,

"Thanks." He turned his head toward Gloria, behind him. "Let's go."

The man rolled his eyes and returned to figuring out the papers on his desk.

Gloria, Jenny, and Earl found their way back along the hall. Earl looked across the lobby to the familiar door. "Hey, College, see how many paces there are between this corner of the wall and that door."

She looked puzzled but did what he asked. She counted off her paces out loud. ". . . Twelve . . . thirteen . . . fourteen."

Earl clapped his hands together. "Fourteen. Now, how many paces between the door and the next door down that hall?"

She looked at him then at Gloria. Then Jenny shrugged and did as he asked. ". . Eighteen . . . nineteen . . . twenty. Now what?"

Earl motioned for her to come back and to open the meeting room door for him. He stopped just inside the doorway, stretching an open palm toward the wall on the left. Then he turned to his right and stretched an open palm that direction. "We need to figure out the number of paces to this room. From this wall to that wall."

Gloria said, "I don't think you're doing it right."

"Of course we are," Earl said.

The stern voice of a woman called out, "May I help you?" Earl turned to see Sheree Jackson, the woman from the event Saturday. "This room is supposed to be closed off."

Jenny pointed in the direction of the office. "The manager said you don't —"

Earl cut her off. "Deputy Fisher allowed us in here earlier. Now, you were in charge of the event here, right? With the psychic and all that?"

The woman scowled, hands on her hips. "I'm the activities director. Or at least, I was. I came back to . . . well, it's none of your business, actually, why I'm here."

"Ah." Earl nodded. "Well, maybe some introductions are in order. My name is Earl Walker, and these are —"

"Visitors are not allowed in here."

He cleared his throat. "Did you see anything unusual that morning?"

The woman checked her watch then folded her arms. "The entire event was unusual. This is not a facility that normally has outside events like that."

"Why did you schedule it? As activities director, I would assume you were in —"

"It was a favor for my dear friend." Her face softened, her eyes moistening. "And then that, that horrible reverend had to . . ."

She covered her mouth with a hand.

Earl noticed Gloria stiffen. He shot her a glance to cool it. He turned back to Ms. Jackson. "All right, even given the unusual circumstances, surely you still had some expectations. Was there anything in particular that went wrong? Or which simply stood out to you? Anything at all?"

The woman stared, her jaw set. "No."

Earl pressed ahead. "Do you know anyone who wanted to see Montague Black dead?"

Her face gnarled. "The sheriff caught the murderer! A hundred people witnessed the whole thing!"

Earl waved it away. "I was here. We were all out in the lobby. But what happened in here" — he held out his hands to indicate the room they were in — "happened behind a closed door."

The woman scrunched her forehead in thought. "But . . . but . . ."

"Tell me something — if I want to get from this room into another room in the building, what are my options?"

The woman took in a deep breath and let it out in a huff. "You can go out those glass doors to the garden. Or you can go out this door to the lobby."

"No secret doors? Secret panels?"

"What?"

"Maybe some way through the fireplace or through the ceiling?"

"What, into the room upstairs? What is it with you people? First, that deputy asks a lot of weird questions. . . ." Ms. Jackson recovered. "No. No secret doors."

Earl nodded. "And if I go to the garden, how do I leave the premises then?"

The woman thought about it. "You either come back in these glass doors, or you go back in through the library."

"You mean the media room?"

She frowned. "Who did you say you were again?"

"Why did you set up the meeting between Montague Black and Pastor Benton?"

"One of them contacted me."

"Who called you? Specifically?"

She hesitated. "I — I was contacted by someone from Pastor Benton's office. I suppose they set it up with —"

Earl raised a hand. "You engineered the entire thing, didn't you?"

The woman's eyes widened. "W–what?"

"I happen to know you were in here near the time of the murder."

"Of course I was — I work here! I mean, I —"

"I can place you out in that garden around the time of the murder. And there was that fight with Black — because he broke up with you."

"Well, that was just —"

"Are you going to tell us the truth, or are we going to go to the police with what we know?" Earl kept a straight face, hoping she wouldn't call his bluff.

The woman tried to stand cold. But her lip trembled, and then her face fell. "I didn't mean for anything to happen to Monty."

Earl raised an eyebrow. "Monty?"

On the verge of tears, she nodded. She bit her lip. "His stage name is — was — Montague Black. I knew him as Monty Schwartz. But that was a long time ago."

"And you wanted to see him again. . . ."

"We had lost touch. Now that he was the big celebrity psychic, he wouldn't have anything to do with me. But I thought if I . . . if the facility . . ." She sniffled. "So I called the pastor's office and said that Monty wanted a meeting . . . and then called Monty's office and said the opposite."

"So you set up the meeting to be here. And how did Black react when he saw you here?"

"He wasn't happy. He figured out I'd set all this up just to see him. It put him in that foul mood of his."

"So you'd say your reunion went poorly?"

She nodded. Her eyes flashed with panic. "Hey, you're not going to saddle me with this, are you? I didn't have anything to gain by killing him!"

"I don't know, a crime of passion . . ."

"If you're going to point a finger, point it at that TV woman!"

Earl raised an eyebrow. "Ms. Zuniga? What did she do?"

"She was about to lose her big TV series. Monty was about to sign with another network and walk out on his contract with her."

"Surely he couldn't just —"

"Apparently he could. I saw them arguing about it that morning."

A man in a black suit and dark glasses was at the door. "Ms. Jackson? We're ready to see you now." The man popped back out. Whether he noticed the others or not was hidden by the glasses.

"I — I have to go."

"What's that? Your exit interview?"

"No, that's the FBI. They're here about the serial killer."

Chapter Eleven

Out in Gloria's car, they regrouped as they watched an ever-growing number of government-issued sedans pull into the parking lot of the facility. Each driver parked as close to the entrance as possible, blocking all the appropriately parked cars in the area.

"Hey," Gloria started, "what was all that in there? About you proving she was in there and all?"

"That was her candy wrapper I found out there in the garden."

"But she worked here. Couldn't she have just as likely —"

"I just wanted to see if she'd panic." Earl noticed Gloria and Jenny both staring back, mouths open. "Well, it worked, didn't it?"

Sheriff Meyer pulled up in a squad car. Blocked by the black sedans, he had to park farther away. As the sheriff and the others exited their cars and made their way to the entrance, Earl noted how harried the sheriff looked. Just a few days earlier, when he appeared on the television news, he had looked so much more in control. Now, he just looked old and tired.

"No wonder he won't listen," Earl grumbled to himself. "He's got more important things to worry about."

"What do you mean?" Gloria's hands were on the steering wheel, her knuckles white.

Earl tapped his passenger window. "I was just saying —"

Jenny opened her door and shot out of the car. She called out to Sheriff Meyer, who turned — as did all the federal agents, several of whom reached inside their suits. Earl hoped none of them were easily startled.

Jenny and the sheriff exchanged words. She was clearly heated. He was clearly exasperated.

Earl couldn't hear anything through the car window. "How do I roll this thing down?"

Gloria turned the key and lowered his power window. By the time the window was down, Jenny was already trudging back, head down. The sheriff shook his head, speaking to one of the feds as they entered the building.

Jenny got in the backseat and slammed her door. "I thought if I could just speak with him directly . . ." She pouted.

Earl craned his neck around. "What'd he say?"

"He said the district attorney has all he needs." She sat back in the seat. "He claimed they're too busy to entertain any theories about ghosts."

"Ghosts?" Earl chuckled. "I guess the deputy has been sharing his theories that Black pulled off his disappearing trick through supernatural means."

Gloria looked at him. "And what do you think?"

"I want something we can take to a jury. And I don't think séances are admissible as evidence." Earl looked out the window, shaking his head. "All things being equal, the sheriff might have been open to rethinking the evidence, but he's got all these government agents underfoot. I'm sure that it's more than a little humiliating."

The car was still idling. Gloria asked, "What now?"

Earl shut his eyes and rubbed his forehead. "The problem is that everything I know is pointing in one direction, and the facts are pointing in another."

"Hey." Jenny leaned on the front seat.

"What if we talked to Bob MacGregor?"

Earl looked at Gloria. "Do I know a Bob MacGregor?"

"He's a deacon at church."

Jenny pulled out her cell phone. "He's also an expert on the occult."

The MacGregors lived in a lovely one-story, redbrick house in an immaculately kept suburban neighborhood. Earl, Gloria, and Jenny arrived to meet with Mr. MacGregor after dinner. Earl judged him to be in his forties, with thinning salt-and-pepper hair. He was dressed in a flannel shirt and chinos.

It took some bit of maneuvering to get Earl's wheelchair over the threshold and inside the front door. Once he was in, Earl shook MacGregor's hand. "Thank you for seeing us."

MacGregor awkwardly indicated Earl's wheelchair. "I'd offer to take you to the study, but it's downstairs and . . . well . . ."

Earl waved a hand. "This is fine."

As the four of them settled into the living room, Earl noticed a lot of blue — blue knickknacks, blue doilies, blue blankets over a blue couch and blue chairs. If they weren't at least all different shades of blue, he might have gotten dizzy.

Earl parked his wheelchair on the far side

of the couch, and the aroma of a recently finished dinner wafted past. Liver and onions.

Mrs. MacGregor offered to make coffee. Earl would have preferred peppermint tea, but he wanted to be polite.

After his wife left them to their visit, MacGregor put his hands on his knees. "Well, young Jenny here said on the phone this had something to do with Pastor Benton . . . ?"

The women looked at Earl. So Earl said, "Um, yes. We're here to ask your advice. See, we were at the nursing home when the murder took place." He cleared his throat. "I understand you're some kind of expert."

MacGregor gasped. "What, in murder?"

"Oh! No — in the supernatural. There's this whole strange component to the murder that has all of us baffled." The other man nodded, waiting for Earl to elaborate. Earl glanced at Gloria and Jenny, to see whether either of them had anything to add. They both stared at him. He turned back to MacGregor. "Something happened in that room. Before Pastor Benton was arrested, he told us —"

"You got to speak to him?"

"Yes. He told us he had been alone in that room, which, if true, means Montague

Black had somehow disappeared."

"But the news reported —"

"That there was a body in the room, yes. But we" — he indicated himself, Gloria, and Jenny — "believe something had to have happened in that room. Maybe something supernatural, maybe some kind of trickery."

"I see." MacGregor considered Earl's words. "I've got to tell you, this was not what I expected. The way the story has been passed around at church . . ." He stopped himself, shaking his head. "I'm afraid I've been listening to gossips." He put one hand on his heart, the other in the air, and turned his eyes upward. "Forgive me, Lord, for bearing false witness." He turned to Earl again, focused. "Please tell me what you know."

Earl shared everything they had seen and heard since the previous Saturday morning. At various intervals, Gloria and Jenny chipped in. To Earl's embarrassment, Jenny even shared what they had learned about so-called "locked-room murders" and "impossible crimes."

Mrs. MacGregor returned with coffee. Earl had his black, Gloria took hers with some sugar, and Jenny accepted cream and sugar. Mr. MacGregor had some peppermint tea.

Finally, they had all finished recounting the previous three days. "So," Earl said to MacGregor, "we've come to you for help. I've heard you have some knowledge in the field of these supernatural things."

The man held out his hands. "Any way I can be of help."

"First of all . . ." Earl gulped down his embarrassment and spit it out. "Can this man, Black, have had legitimate 'psychic' powers?"

MacGregor sat back in his chair and crossed his legs. He folded his arms and touched an index finger to his lips. "Well, Mr. Walker —"

"Call me Earl."

"All right, Earl, the Bible says there are spiritual forces in the world. But it strongly condemns psychics, tarot cards, mediums, horoscopes, spiritism, astrology, fortune-tellers, palm readers, séances, the occult — all that stuff."

"It says all that in the Bible?"

"Sure does." He thought for a second. "Let's see . . . Leviticus 20:27 . . . Deuteronomy 18:10–13 . . ." MacGregor stood up, left the room for a moment, and brought back a Bible. He began to flip through it. "These practices all stem from the belief that there are spiritual beings — gods, spirits, the ghosts of our loved ones — who will give us advice and guidance."

Earl glanced over at Gloria and then Jenny, both of whom listened intently. Earl looked at MacGregor. "But what if you're using these powers for good? I mean, this character was helping the police. And now that he's dead, they had to call in the FBI. . . ."

"God makes no distinction between so-called 'white magic' and 'black magic.' All magic is sorcery in His eyes — and scripture explicitly forbids it." He flipped to a place in his Bible. "Acts 19:19 describes how the people who practiced magic brought their books together and began burning them after they had put their trust in Jesus."

"Can I see that?"

MacGregor handed the Bible to Earl, pointing to a specific passage. As Earl skimmed, he continued. "There are several examples where someone practiced the occult arts but could not perform at the same level as those who trusted in God. In Exodus, chapter eight, you have Pharaoh's priests, who couldn't match God's power as demonstrated through Moses. In the book of Daniel, you have the magicians who could not interpret the king's dreams — but

Daniel was successful where they failed, because his power came from God."

"Okay, if I understand this — and, keep in mind, this is all new to me — the Bible says the supernatural world does exist: There are supernatural *powers;* there are supernatural *beings. . . .*"

"That's right. And regular human beings can connect with that power. Some of it is good, and some of it is evil. If you're tapped into the supernatural and it isn't God, then you're actually working with demons."

Earl raised his eyebrows. "You're saying those are real?"

"The Bible says they are. That's why the fourth chapter of First John says to 'try the spirits.' We can't tell just by looking at them."

"Really?"

"In fact, it's a sin to assume something is demonic or Christian without testing the spirits. Because with our eyes and our physical senses, they all look the same to us. Only an idiot thinks he can tell the difference without testing it by the light of scripture."

"Uh-huh." Earl rubbed his eyes. This was a lot of information for a new churchgoer to take in at once.

"There was a fortune-teller in the book of Acts, chapter sixteen — here it is — who could predict the future, until the apostle Paul rebuked a demon out of her. And here in Second Corinthians, chapter eleven, it says 'Satan himself is transformed into an angel of light. Therefore it is no great thing if his ministers also be transformed as the ministers of righteousness; whose end shall be according to their works.' "

"But I remember Pastor Benton mentioning something about the guy could be just a con artist. How about that? Can you fake this stuff?"

"Absolutely. There are several methods that can be employed to give the impression that one can see the future or tell fortunes. For starters, there is theatricality: the words, the look, the manner. . . ." MacGregor sat back in his chair. "You set out the tarot cards, you have the trick lighting, you wear certain things that make you look and seem more authentic, depending on the kind of image you're trying to project."

"I think Black had some kind of stage show."

"Oh . . . in that case, while the so-called 'psychic' is out of the room or offstage, the crew member or helper is probably having a very pointed conversation with the intended victim, asking a lot of personal information. At some point the helper secretly passes on that information. And then the 'mystic' reveals the information during the act, and everyone is amazed."

Gloria leaned forward. "I've seen something like that before, where the assistant talks to the audience member, but he never even goes near the magician to talk to him. How do they do that?"

MacGregor nodded. "Generally, they use a microphone-and-earpiece setup. The psychic seems too far away to hear you whispering to the assistant, but you're actually speaking into a hidden microphone. He hears every word in his tiny earpiece."

Earl chuckled. "That one I learned from watching *Columbo*."

Jenny asked, "What about the smaller-scale deal? Like a local fortune-teller working out of her home?"

"When you call ahead to make an appointment, your number pops up on her caller ID. That's all she needs to go online and research you ahead of time. The *'psychic'* or *'medium'* can find all kinds of your personal information through completely natural — if dishonest — means."

Gloria tilted her head. "How about that."

But MacGregor wasn't finished. "And then you have cold readings — where it's just you and the 'psychic,' like you just walk up and he or she starts telling you all kinds of stuff they just *couldn't* have known ahead of time."

Earl asked, "You're going to tell us that's a trick, too?"

The man nodded, grinning. "Some educated guesswork and asking a lot of questions. There are certain ways he can phrase his statements so they seem to apply to you — but, of course, he's being so general, they apply to almost *anyone.* Statistically, he'll eventually touch some nerve that makes you think he knows what he's talking about. It only takes one small guess that hits its mark, and then the victim does all the heavy lifting." MacGregor sat back in his chair. "Even when you know it's all a fake, a good performance can still be quite convincing."

Jenny wrinkled her nose. "So, the trick is he's just a good listener?"

"It does take a lot of educated listening. The so-called *'psychic'* tries to be as vague as possible and let the victim lead the conversation. Even if the psychic is on the wrong track, the victim often assumes he had it right. All the while, he keeps watching for certain cues and feedback. He makes some guesses, and he keeps going when he misses. The psychic just tells the victim what they want to hear — the trick is to be positive but vague."

Gloria gasped. "So there's nothing to it."

MacGregor leaned forward. "Please don't get me wrong — whether or not this man used demonic powers or simply faked it, what's really at stake is how *you* respond to it. By opening yourself to these occult strategies, you're turning away from God and putting your faith in counterfeits. False gods. And you're opening your heart and your mind to all sorts of spiritual oppression."

Earl coughed into his hand. "Getting back to the problem of the locked room, let me see if I understand what you're saying. If we can't find some natural explanation for how Black got out of that room, then we might conclude these demonic forces gave him the power to somehow vanish or dematerialize or whatever you call it."

"I don't know about that. Now, there are several examples of somebody appearing or disappearing by the power of God." MacGregor got his Bible again, flipping through it. "We have Enoch in Genesis, chapter five; Elijah in Second Kings, chapter two; Jesus in Luke, chapter twenty-four; Philip in Acts, chapter eight. . . ."

He looked up from his Bible. "Throughout the Bible, we see the devil and the demons doing their best to counterfeit the works of God and of Christ and of the Holy Spirit. But there are *no* examples of the devil able to make a person physically appear or disappear."

"So this Black faked it somehow."

"He must have. Of course, that would actually be an *'illusion,'* which is actually not occult. In fact, it's not even *'psychic.'* "

"What's the difference?"

"It's a skill, like any physical stunt or feat, which, of course, is all fine in the eyes of God, as long as you're not glorifying the devil. So, it's okay to go to church and be an illusionist."

Earl scratched his nose. "Hmm."

Gloria asked, "What are you thinking?"

"How will any of this convince a jury the pastor is innocent?"

Chapter Twelve

The next morning, Earl was alone at home. He sipped his coffee, trying to fight his way to consciousness. He'd stayed up way past his bedtime, reading.

The TV was on, tuned to the local news, the sound muted. Earl paid little attention to the flickering images, busy mulling over the events of the previous few days.

To think, just one week earlier, he was trying to figure out how to have a heart-to-heart talk with the widow Gloria Logan. And then all this other stuff happened.

Truth to tell, Earl still didn't know what he believed about the murder of Montague Black. The fate of Pastor Benton would soon be in the hands of the district attorney and at the mercy of a jury of his peers. With all the publicity surrounding the murder and the arrest, and Pastor Benton's own church all but ready to proclaim his guilt to the world, one had to wonder whether he could even get a fair trial.

Earl turned his attention to the stacks of library books on his coffee table. The night before, he had sampled a few of the titles. Earl was not much for fiction, but he found the Agatha Christie titles weren't bad. He stayed up way too late reading *The ABC Murders.* However, even after he got to the end, Earl didn't think it could be considered an "impossible crime" — it must have gotten into Jenny's pile by mistake.

When he glanced back up at the TV, a familiar scene flickered on the screen: Deputy Fisher leading a handcuffed Pastor Benton to the patrol car. Earl turned up the sound.

". . . since the death of Montague Black. TV producer Divina Zuniga says she is editing together the package as a tribute. Black was scheduled to star in his own syndicated talk show, produced by Zuniga, this fall."

The TV picture changed now to the newscaster. A square floating over his shoulder bore the legend, SERIAL KILLER? "Meanwhile, the sheriff's office continues to investigate a recent series of deaths in Mt. Hermit. Without the help of celebrated psychic Montague Black, the sheriff has called in help from the FBI."

The screen now showed Sheriff Meyer

awash in government agents, investigators, forensic specialists, what have you. Earl wondered what in the world the specialists would find after all this time. After all, the crime scene — the woman's bedroom — was no doubt all trampled over by now.

But then, that was their expertise. As Earl reminded himself, he was just a crippled old ex-bus driver in a wheelchair.

Taking another sip of his coffee, Earl had to admit he really didn't know what the crime scene was like. After all, that was a completely different murder — and in someone's residential room, far away from the public thoroughfare of a lobby.

The two deaths, Cloris Thomas's and Black's were completely unrelated. Just a weird coincidence, but that's all it was. Right?

The phone rang. Earl got it on the third ring. "Hello?"

"Good morning."

"Gloria! What are you doing?"

"I was just taking my morning break, and I thought I would see how you're doing."

"Just having some coffee and watching the news."

"Did you eat any breakfast?"

Earl paused. "I was about to. I got side-tracked."

"All right." There was a muffled voice on her end, someone else, and Gloria answered them. Then she got back on the phone. "So, anyway, I'm only working a half day. If you wanted me to come over for lunch . . ." There was a hesitation on the other end. "I could."

Earl took a breath. "Sure. How about you come over, and we can talk about our plans then. For the afternoon." *Or for the rest of our lives,* Earl thought. *Whatever works for you.*

"Sounds great! Then I'll see you after — oh! I have to go. 'Bye. Love you!" She hung up.

Earl stared at the receiver in his hand. *"Love you"?* He carefully hung up the phone, thinking over every word of the conversation.

Gloria had said she loved him. Or did she? Was it said as a casual conversation-ender? She'd never ended a conversation like that before.

What did it mean?

It was getting on toward lunchtime. Earl's hands trembled as he tried to figure out what to serve. There wasn't much in the cupboard — of course, what little he had was because Gloria insisted on helping with shopping for groceries. She did not approve of an exclusive diet of all things boxed, canned, or frozen.

Notwithstanding, all he could think to offer was a boxed fried rice dinner. Everything was right there in the box: can of chicken, vegetables, and broth; bag of rice; pouch of Asian seasoning.

Best of all, it was fast, and it would keep. Gloria hadn't mentioned what time she'd be over. If he shot for noon, it wouldn't matter whether he made the fried rice too soon or too late. It was all good.

Plus, it was an easy dish to make. Just pour the ingredients in the skillet and forget about it for fifteen minutes, which gave him plenty of time to worry about whether or not Gloria had, in fact, said she loved him.

As he set the table, he couldn't help but fumble with the silverware. If Gloria had genuinely expressed love for him — in the way that he loved her — then the talk about their "relationship" would likely be painless. Well, mostly.

On the other hand, if she considered her friendship with Earl to be so platonic that she could refer to "love" so casually — well, the aforementioned talk would not go well at all. That prospect paralyzed Earl.

Suddenly, the distraction of meddling in a

murder case didn't seem like such a bad idea, which is why, when there was a ring of the bell and a knock on the door, and then Gloria was in his apartment, Earl decided to take the coward's way out. He would do everything possible to keep their conversation focused on the plight of Pastor Benton.

When she arrived, Gloria was stiff and awkward. "Oh, something smells . . . Chinese."

"It's fried rice." Avoiding her eyes, Earl went to check the stove. "It should be ready in a few minutes. Have a seat."

"How was your . . . morning?"

"Fine. And . . . yours?"

"Fine."

"Nothing special happened? At the office, I mean?"

"Not at the office. Why, did something special happen here?"

"No! That is, I was just watching the news. And I'm a little out of sorts because I stayed up late reading one of the books College left."

"Oh? Really?"

"Yeah. It, um, really gave me some ideas regarding this Pastor Benton thing."

"It did?"

"Yes." Actually, it hadn't. "I was just thinking about how we need to press on and see what we can do about Pastor Benton."

Gloria let out a big sigh. "You think so? I mean —"

"Oops! There goes the timer! Hold that thought." Earl wheeled himself back to the kitchen.

She called after him, "Want any help?"

"No! I mean, I got it." Reaching up for the skillet, he burned his hand. He bit his lip and grabbed the pot holder. He moved the skillet to a different burner and switched the stove off. He took a fork and stirred the watery rice concoction. He'd expected something a little different. But he guessed that's what he got when it came out of a box.

He grabbed a big spoon then remembered that the plates were out on the table. He set the spoon on the edge of the skillet, but it fell to the floor, splattering Asian seasoned water on his pants.

Gloria called from the other room, "Are you all right?"

Earl rubbed his forehead. "If you wouldn't mind bringing the plates in here. I forgot what I was doing and . . ." He took a deep breath. He let it out.

"Here you are." Gloria set the plates on the counter.

"If you want to grab a spoon out of the

drawer there." He reached for the one on the floor. "I've got a mess to clean up down here."

"Here, hon — er, let me help you. Why don't you just go in the other room and relax."

Earl hesitated. He felt light-headed. Finally, he decided maybe it was best to just let her handle it.

Parking at the dinette table, Earl started praying like silent gangbusters — for wisdom, for direction, for rescue . . . anything to untangle the knots in his stomach.

Gloria returned to the table, setting a plate of fried rice concoction out for each of them. "Looks great!"

"Well." Earl twitched. "It came out of a box." He grabbed a fork and started to jab at his food before he caught himself. "Oh. Wait." He set the fork on the table and reached out for Gloria's hand without thinking.

His hand was out there a fleeting second before he realized this was the first he'd tried to hold her hand, even if only for prayer, since she may (or may not) have said she loved him. His arm flinched. He almost pulled his hand back, but he didn't want to be rude. So the hand was still there when Gloria tentatively took it.

They closed their eyes and bowed their heads. "Lord," Earl prayed, "we just want to thank You for this day. And for this food. Please bless it." He paused. A dozen words came to mind, a hundred. He wasn't comfortable saying any of them. Then he thought of Pastor Benton, sitting all alone in that jail cell. "Please help us figure out this thing. You know what happened. Please help everyone down here to know, too."

Together they said, "Amen." Their hands parted. Earl couldn't decide whether or not Gloria's hand had lingered.

Earl ignored the flutter in his chest and attacked his fried rice with savagery. Mouth full, chewing, he kept his eyes on the plate. He said, "So, like I was saying, I had a few thoughts regarding Pastor Benton."

"Oh. Yes." She sounded tired.

He looked up then swallowed. "What?"

"I'm just starting to wonder if we're wasting our time."

"But you were his champion. I thought you were certain he is innocent."

"Oh, don't get me wrong — of course he's innocent." She looked down, picking at her fried rice with her fork. "But all those professionals, with their equipment, their resources . . ." She looked at him. "What can we really do?"

"You sound like me."

"Well, maybe you were right. Maybe it's time we stop trying to somehow undo the case with the sheriff and focus our attention on the trial."

"They've set a date?"

"I don't think so. But if the police decide he's the murderer, a trial is the next thing, isn't it?"

"I guess so."

"We need to make sure he has a good lawyer. Maybe we could offer to help him." She put an elbow on the table and rested her head on one hand. "Of course, he would say the same thing: 'Leave it to the professionals.' "

"Yes. Professionals." He pushed his plate back, unfinished. "You know what I think? The police are so mesmerized by this other case — this serial killer thing — they just don't want to rethink something like the murder of Montague Black. If the sheriff had a chance to stop and think about it — or if he knew what we knew —"

Tears came to her eyes. With her voice cracking, she asked, "What *do* we know?"

"Hey, what's this?" He reached out and touched her face, wiping tears off her cheek with his thumb. Their eyes met. She looked very serious. Earl leaned forward, cupped her face in his hands, and kissed her tenderly on the nose.

He sat back in the chair. He tried to think of a way to articulate what had just happened. Instead, he said, "What we know is that Pastor Benton couldn't have killed that man. Somehow, someway, somebody else killed Montague Black." Earl cleared his throat. He looked down at his shoes. "As long as the sheriff refuses to acknowledge that fact, we are apparently the only ones willing to ferret out the real truth."

Earl reached out and grabbed Gloria's hand. "I know you're tired. And I know I keep vacillating back and forth on this. But you need to be the anchor. You keep us on track." He offered her a crooked smile. "You keep *me* on track."

Gloria returned the smile, her mood lighter now. "Don't you think maybe we should talk about what happened just now?"

"We need to help Pastor Benton while we can. You gotta make hay while it's still daylight."

"Chicken."

Earl gave her a cockeyed smile. "Yes."

Gloria squeezed his hand. "Fine. So, what do we do now?"

"On the news before, they were talking about that TV producer lady."

"Ms. Zuniga?"

"That's the one. If Ms. Jackson can be believed, then Ms. Zuniga could have some very interesting things to tell us."

Chapter Thirteen

It took a bit of research to figure out how to track down Divina Zuniga. They couldn't find her name in the phone book, and there weren't many television studios in the Yellow Pages.

Finally, after several phone calls, Gloria spoke with a person at a television station who told her to call another person, who in turn told her to call someone else. That person did not have Ms. Zuniga's contact information, but he knew someone who did.

Finally, Gloria reached the offices where Ms. Zuniga worked, First Film and Sound Design. "Okay, here's the thing," she told Earl. "I talked with someone at the front desk. Ms. Zuniga cannot take any calls, because she's busy in one of the editing bays, whatever that means. The young man thinks Ms. Zuniga is likely to be around the offices for the next several hours." She dug in her purse for her keys and her driving glasses. "Let's go!"

On the drive over, Earl said, "You know, I've been thinking . . ."

"Yes?" There was a lilt in her voice. It was nice.

"One of the roadblocks that keeps tripping us up is this disappearing business. If we believe the pastor —"

"And we do."

"— then this man was gone. From the room, I mean. And unless the answer is that *'suicide'* theory — and I don't think either of us buys that — then we also have to wonder about a third person who either appeared or disappeared from there, too."

Gloria kept her eyes on the road. "But we couldn't find any secret doors."

"Sure. But I was thinking about what your deacon said about it being a skill. And I would think that the good illusionists would have some idea how to do it without a secret door."

"Okay . . . and that would be how . . . ?"

"First of all, I guess, you have your basic mirrors."

"But we looked for those, too. Didn't we? Wasn't that why Jenny looked up the chimney?"

"Yeah." Earl looked out his passenger window. "But all Jenny's talk about 'locked rooms' and 'impossible crimes' and such made me think about the old show *Mission: Impossible.*"

Gloria glanced over at Earl then back at the road. "I remember that show. Dwight and I used to watch it. But what does that have to with this? You think this Montague Black character was secretly a spy?"

"Well, no . . ."

"Oh! And that's how he was getting all that information about the serial killer. He was using some kind of spy technology to record —"

"He was not a spy." Earl took a breath. "Think about what College was saying. Think about the concept of the so-called 'impossible crime.' Then think about the old *Mission: Impossible* — listen to the name: *'Impossible.'* And every week, they had to figure out a way to break into some impregnable place, hoodwink some dictator or crime boss, and then get away without being caught."

She seemed doubtful. "All right."

"Sure, it was just a television show, but it gives us some idea of the possibilities."

"Here we are." Gloria pulled into a parking lot. Earl looked up at the sign on the side of the building, FIRST FILM AND SOUND DESIGN. Gloria switched off the ignition. "Do we know what we're going to ask her?"

Earl took a breath. "I guess the first thing is to find out whether she'll even talk to us. After that, we see how it goes."

"Because that's worked so well for us so far."

"I do believe my cynicism is rubbing off on you."

Gloria gave him a tender smile. She reached over and touched his hand. Then she got out of the car, got his wheelchair out of the trunk, and came around for him.

As they headed for the entrance, Earl said, "I remember an episode of *Mission: Impossible* where Barney had to hide inside the house of this mobster. He had this reflective curtain that hooked to the legs of a corner table, so he curled up behind it, and no one could see him."

"How does that keep someone from knowing you're there? What is it reflecting?"

"Well, it was kind of like this. . . ." Earl made a motion with his hands, frowned, and made another motion. "Well, it was hooked diagonally so that —"

"Wouldn't it have to look like the end of the table?"

Earl didn't answer. He noticed that several

cars in the parking lot looked awfully familiar.

At the entrance, Gloria held the door, while Earl pushed himself through. Inside, the man behind the desk told them to have a seat and wait. Gloria sat on a black vinyl-covered couch. Earl squeezed his wheelchair between a couple of chairs. He glanced at the magazines on the glass table. They all seemed to focus on television and film, but purely from a technical point of view.

He looked at Gloria. She stared back, smiling. He blushed. "Um . . ."

"So, you were talking about the man under the end table. He was invisible?"

"Not exactly invisible." Earl locked his fingers together. "That is, no more so than my standing behind that wall over there makes me invisible. I mean, you can't see me, but it's because I'm behind something." He sat back in his wheelchair and locked his fingers behind his head.

Gloria shook her head. "When we were talking about the furniture before, I thought we were trying to find a wardrobe or a big chest of drawers. Something big."

"If there was some way to curl up under that writing desk." Earl sat forward, hands on his knees. "And if you had some sort of cloth or wrap or something that hides you."

"You keep talking like you can't hide behind the couch. But what if —"

"Then who was back there? If there's someone behind the couch, where did he go? Whoever it was certainly wasn't hiding back behind the couch when the sheriff ran in there to find the body. He would have had nowhere to run but back out into the lobby. And even if Black hid behind the couch, and he popped out to scare the pastor . . . well, that still doesn't help us, does it?"

Gloria sighed. She thought for a second, and then her eyes lit up. "How about if the murder weapon was dropped into the room from *outside.* Maybe there was a hole in thc ceiling, and they threw the —"

Earl shook his head. "Too complicated. If we can believe the pastor, the victim wasn't in the room. Then, in the space of a few seconds, the killer materialized, deposited the dead body, and then disappeared again."

"So, not the mirrors. But there must be other ways of hiding. On *Mission: Impossible* they used costumes and sleight of hand and big, explosive diversions."

Earl cracked a grin, nodding. "You're right! They created illusions. What if this Montague Black created the illusion he wasn't in that room?"

"You said something about a curtain."

"Sure."

"Well . . . ?"

Earl took a deep breath. He glanced at the guy behind the desk then down the hall behind the desk. Then he looked back at Gloria. "Well, I don't know. Maybe we should go talk to a professional."

"Do you know any professional magicians?"

"We could look them up."

"You think they're in the Yellow Pages?"

Earl shrugged. "Why not?"

She considered this. "Yeah, I guess why not?"

The conversation faded out as they continued waiting. Earl glanced at the magazines again. They didn't hold any more interest now for him than they did the last time he looked. He heard the hum of a microwave and the sound of popping.

He turned back to Gloria. "Maybe a practiced illusionist would know how to use a curtain that matches the pattern on the carpet or something. And when you're under it and you're very still, maybe a person in the room would miss seeing you."

"So, Montague Black was hiding under this magical curtain? Or are you talking about the real killer?"

"I'm not saying that's what they did, but a professional stage magician might be able to explain how to do it."

They were silent again. Nobody came to see them.

A man in a black suit and dark glasses came in from the parking lot. He glanced in the direction of Earl and Gloria and stopped a second. His eyes were hidden behind the glasses. He turned to the kid behind the desk, nodded curtly, and entered the back hall. He took a door to the left and was gone.

Nothing else happened for several minutes. The smell of burned popcorn floated through the air.

Earl said, "I'm just saying, an illusionist has a lot of tools at his disposal, when you think about it."

"Uh-huh."

"We were so focused on the architecture of the room that we didn't think about all the ways a man could create an illusion without the benefit of secret panels."

"Okay."

"The illusion is created through misdirection, through costumes, through the clothing, with the use of assistants . . . and, I guess, trapdoors." Earl stopped. "Come to think of it, it's a lot like what the deacon was saying about one of those fake psychics. It's all an illusion."

"Mm-hmm."

"Of course, there's a big difference between a person pretending to be a psychic and a person performing an illusion. An illusionist *tells* you it's an illusion. The fake psychic tries to get his hooks in you."

Gloria nodded, her eyes starting to glaze over. "I see."

"But we keep going in circles with this thing. We're so focused on the *how* that we forget to ask the *who.*" Earl rubbed his hands together. "It's not enough to find someone who might have wanted to get Montague Black out of the way. We have to find someone who could appear in a locked room, deposit a dead body, and disappear again. All in the space of less than a minute."

The door opened, and Deputy Fisher entered, carrying several brown bags. When he saw Earl and Gloria, he frowned. "Don't you folks have anything better to do?"

Earl put on his best *Who, me?* look. "We have as much right to be here as anywhere."

"You don't have the right to harass people."

"These people are free to answer or not answer our questions. If they choose to refuse to answer our questions and thereby look guilty —"

"There! That's what I'm talking about. You cannot go around falsely accusing people of crimes. You need to have a badge to do that."

"So . . . a badge gives you a right to falsely accuse people?"

The deputy's cheeks reddened. "I didn't mean it like that." He turned to the man at the desk and set the bags down. "Here. Tell Special Agent Fletcher" — he paused, casting a glance over his shoulder and dropped his voice — "his lunch is here."

Earl held his tongue. He felt pity for the deputy.

Deputy Fisher came over. "Look, folks, I don't want the reverend to be in jail, either. But if that psychic fella transported outta that room by some supernatural means, the only way we can clear the reverend's name is to somehow prove it can be done."

Earl raised an eyebrow. "You think so?"

"Sure!" The deputy leaned in and spoke in a low voice. "You folks'll be glad to know I have been quietly pursuing that very line of investigation."

"To prove the victim had the ability to *'transport'* himself from one location to another."

"Yes."

Gloria muttered, "Well!"

Earl asked, "How do you account for the knife?"

The deputy pushed his hat back. "Well, if one can do it, then so can two. Or, for that matter, the knife itself might have been transported from outside the room."

Gloria asked, "Into the man's back?"

"Ayup." The deputy paused. "Well, he was stabbed in the chest."

Earl asked, "And how do you pursue an inquiry like that?"

"I've put calls into several experts. I only need one willing to go on record with a judge."

"And by *'experts'* you mean . . . ?"

"Mediums. Spirits. Psychics. You know, folks able to demonstrate how a murder weapon — or a body — can be mentally transported over some great distance."

Earl nodded dreamily. "Wow."

The deputy grinned. "I knew you folks would understand. We've just gotta get unbelievers like Sheriff Meyer to —"

He was cut off when his walkie-talkie sputtered. "Fisher!"

The deputy's face fell, and he grabbed the device off his belt. "Yes, sir?"

"Where's lunch?"

Deputy Fisher's eyes went wide. They all

looked at the desk, where the bags still sat. The kid manning the station was apparently too busy with his phone call to have passed along the deputy's message.

Fisher spoke into the walkie-talkie. "I just got here, Sheriff. I'm on the way back there now." The young man replaced the device on his belt. "The sheriff hasn't been himself since the feds flew in. It's like they've been constantly . . ." He stopped himself. "I'm sorry. I guess I have no business burdening you poor folks with it."

Earl asked, "Why are they having lunch here? Is this a command post or something?"

"What? Oh no, they're watching footage of the deal from Saturday."

"I thought the FBI was looking for the serial killer."

"Okay, first of all, it's not officially classified as a 'serial killer' case. Second, they think the serial killer might have been at the meeting between Benton and Black."

Gloria let out an "Oh!"

"They got a profiler watching raw video footage to see whether anyone in the crowd looks suspicious."

Earl thought back to the assemblage of weirdos who'd been there. If the FBI profiler had to pick a specific sicko out of that group, Earl didn't envy him at all.

Deputy Fisher tipped his hat to Gloria, grabbed the bags, and headed down the hall. He disappeared through a door on the left.

Gloria checked her watch. "How much longer do we wait? If the boy at the desk can't be bothered to call back for the deputy, I bet he didn't even tell the young lady we're out here."

Earl grunted. "I think you're right."

They went to the parking lot. As Gloria was pointing the way to her car, Earl saw an exit door propped open. A woman had her back to the brick wall, smoking a cigarette.

"I think that's her." Earl gripped the rims of his wheels and closed the distance, hoping she wouldn't finish before he got there. As he neared, he called out, "Ms. Zuniga? Divina Zuniga?"

The woman almost dropped her cigarette. "Yes?"

"I saw you Saturday morning."

"Oh. Sure." She dropped the cigarette to the pavement and ground it out with her heel. "If you'll excuse me —"

"We want to ask a couple questions."

Ms. Zuniga motioned to the door. "Actually, my crew is with the —"

"Federal agents. We know. We're also" —

Earl paused — "special investigators."

The woman looked at the two, furrowing her brow. "Really? You don't look like the others."

"Like I said, we're special."

She folded her arms. "What do you want to know?"

"My understanding is you were partners with Montague Black. You were going to produce his television show."

The woman reached into her purse for another cigarette and lit it. "That's right."

"Who do you think had a reason to murder Black?"

"Well, that minister is the one they arrested. You just need one murderer, don't you?"

"But who else had a motive? For example, you were seen arguing with Black that morning. He was planning to break his contract with you because he was offered a better deal, wasn't he?"

Her eyes flashed with anger. "That's none of your business. Who did you say you represent?"

Earl narrowed his eyes. "You were in the room at the time of the murder."

"I was not!"

"I saw you at the door myself."

"I opened the door, sure, but my cameraman grabbed me before I went in. We had an emergency with the equipment."

"Did you look in the room?"

She shrugged. "Black was meditating."

Earl leaned forward in his wheelchair. "Wait — you saw him?"

"Yeah. He was over by the glass doors. He had his head against the door like he was deep in thought. But like I said, I was called away before I had a chance to go in."

Earl sat back again. He started rubbing his chin.

Ms. Zuniga took a puff on her cigarette then dropped it to the pavement and stamped it out. "If you want to find someone with a motive, go talk to Hamilton Page. He's writing a book about this serial killer case."

"I don't see what —"

The woman was kicking the prop away from the open door. "Hamilton needed Montague to sign a release form before he could publish this book."

"And Black refused?"

"You tell me." She closed the door and was gone.

CHAPTER FOURTEEN

Altogether, they must have sat in the car for ten minutes.

Gloria had asked, "So, how do we find this man?"

Earl wasn't sure. "Can't we check around?"

"Well, sure, but check around where? She didn't say he worked at a newspaper or a magazine."

"She didn't say he didn't."

"Well, sure."

"Of course, she didn't say he wasn't a plumber or a bricklayer, either."

"Huh?"

"Nothing. I'm just saying that focusing on what she didn't say doesn't really help us." After some minutes of thinking, Earl hit upon the idea of going to the library. "After all," he said, "if the man writes books, they might have them there. And if they do, maybe one of the librarians knows something about him."

Neither of them could think of a better plan of action, so they headed for the library. Gloria only vaguely knew the way. Of course, Earl had no clue how to get to the library from where they were — or, for that matter, how to get to the library at all — so Gloria had to stop for directions. Twice.

On the way, Gloria asked, "I've been meaning to ask you something."

His heart started pounding. "All right."

"Back there, you claimed we were special investigators. I know you're trying to help Pastor Benton, but that doesn't give us the right to lie to people."

"I wasn't lying. We are special. We are investigators."

"Yes, but —"

"And the deputy himself bestowed on us the rank of 'special investigators.' "

Gloria glanced at him then back at the road. "He did?" "Don't you remember? Back at Heritage Care. He told that groundskeeper that you, me, and College were 'special investigators.' "

"Oh." She seemed relieved. "Okay, then."

"I don't think it comes with benefits or anything. . . ."

"What?"

"Never mind." He looked out the window. They went the rest of the way to the library in silence.

Earl enjoyed being in the car with her. He enjoyed being alone with her. He enjoyed that they didn't need to fill the air with a lot of chatter. Well, not much chatter, anyway. He loved Gloria. Yes, he was sure of it. It had been a long time since he had loved someone, but he was sure this is what it was. And if he could just determine whether or not she loved him, too, everything would be aces.

At the library, they found a librarian who knew true-crime author Hamilton Page by name — mainly because the author himself had visited recently and thrown a fit that the library didn't have any of his books on the shelf.

The man was not a local author. Apparently, he was only in town to follow the " 'serial killer" ' investigation. Even though the sheriff was unwilling to call it a serial killer, the national media had already declared it to be so.

So, Mr. Page was staying in town, but the librarian didn't know where or for how long. He had left a card.

Earl wanted Gloria to call the number. She was so much better at talking to strangers. For that matter, she was so much better talking to anybody. But she was not about to call a strange man, so Earl made the call. He set up an appointment with Page to meet at the motel where he was staying.

Some thirty minutes later, Gloria and Earl pulled into the parking lot. Gloria got Earl's wheelchair out of the trunk, and they worked together to get him into the chair. Earl chided himself for not scheduling the meeting for later, to give them some more time. He hated being late, a prejudice ingrained in him from twenty-five years of driving a metro bus.

Wheeling himself through the sliding doors at the entrance, Earl immediately scanned the small lobby for the man they were meeting. A muscular man in a tight black T-shirt, his head shaved, waved and stood.

Earl and Gloria made their way across to where the man was, Gloria taking a comfortable seat next to him. Earl had some trouble getting his wheelchair past the table but somehow squeezed through.

The man shook hands with them. "I'm glad you could meet with me. I'm Hamilton Page."

"I'm Earl Walker, and this is Gloria Logan." He grumbled, "Sorry we're late."

"That's all right." Page took his chair again. He grabbed a notebook and started flipping through pages of scribbling. "I'm sure you'll be a great help."

Earl and Gloria exchanged a glance. Earl squared his jaw. Had he misunderstood the conversation on the phone?

He cleared his throat. "Actually, we were hoping *you'd* help *us.*"

Page clicked his ballpoint pen. "Really? I don't see how."

"We understand you're writing a book about Montague Black."

"Well, the book is about the 'Mercy Killer,' so I guess —"

"I'm sorry, the what?"

"The 'Mercy Killer.' That's the name of the serial killer."

"It is? You mean he wrote it down somewhere?"

"Well, no. It's not an official name, but it's the code name I'm using for my book. I've sent out a test balloon to some members of the media to see whether it will fly."

Earl was speechless. Gloria said, "Uh-huh."

"When you're working on a media property, the name is so important. If we can come up with just the right name that will capture the spirit of the event . . ."

Earl coughed. "Wait, are we still talking about the serial killer?"

The man nodded. "That used to be enough to sell books and maybe get a TV movie of the week. Now you need a trade name that stands out." He clicked his pen again and started scribbling in his notebook. "Now, Mr. Walker, how are you participating in the investigation to find the Mercy Killer?"

Earl felt his anger rising. "So were these victims terminally ill or something?"

Page shook his head. "They don't seem to mention anything about that."

Earl shifted in his wheelchair. "There's got to be more than that. You don't call him the 'Mercy Killer' for no reason."

"Well, all the victims were old. You know, senior citizens."

Earl squinted an eye at him. "So when you kill a senior citizen, you're doing him some kind of favor?"

Page's eyes grew wide. "No! I never —" He pointed to the paper. "They said it!"

"We old geezers still have a lot to contribute to society."

"Oh I know!"

"Arts, sciences, business. We have the wisdom that comes from experience."

"I know!"

"You college kids with your degrees, you've barely even seen the world —"

Gloria put a hand on his shoulder. She said in a soft voice, "Relax, hon."

Earl grunted. "You're right. I'm sorry." He tapped his fingertips together, waiting for his blood to cool back to the normal temperature. He said, "Anyway, we're not here about the . . . serial killer. We're investigating the murder of Montague Black."

Page stopped scribbling and looked up from his pad, his face betraying disbelief. "Are you kidding? That case is wrapped up. I don't even think I'll be able to get a whole chapter out of it."

"We have reason to believe that new evidence will surface soon." Earl shifted in his wheelchair again. "For starters, you had an argument with Montague Black the morning he was murdered."

"I don't know that I would refer to it as an *'argument'.*"

"Maybe you forget, I was there when you told Carpenter about it."

The man's eyes widened. "I can explain. It's very simple."

"I'm sure it is."

"You see, I flew in to develop my next book around this Mercy —"

"Please stop calling it that."

"The, um, serial killer. The deaths themselves didn't have enough juice, but the channelist angle —"

" '*Juice*'?"

"You know. Sauce. Wallop."

"You mean '*pizzazz*'?"

"Um, sure. I guess."

"So, these people losing their lives isn't enough for your little story? The torment of their families —"

"Hey, man, don't kill the messenger here. I'm all about justice for the little guy, you know, but if the book doesn't sell, I don't get to keep writing books, you know? My publisher says I have to come up with books that have, er, '*pizzazz.*' " Page shrugged and grinned. "Just the way it is."

"I see." Behind Earl, Gloria huffed to herself. He said, "But that doesn't explain the argument."

"Oh. That. Well, when I got here, I found the real hook was the channelist angle — Montague Black was golden."

"So to speak."

"Yes! The serial killer angle was tired, but here was a man who claimed to channel the spirits of the dead. . . ."

"But crackpot psychics do their phony bit with the police all the time."

Page sat back in the chair. "Did you know that before Black came along, nobody even knew these people were murdered?"

"Why, what did he do? Why should the police listen to him?"

"Originally, the official report was that these folks died of natural causes. In their sleep, you know. They were old geezers, so why should —" His eyes widened, and he glanced quickly to Earl and Gloria and back to Earl. "No offense."

Earl raised his hand to pretend there was no offense taken. "So? What did Black do to change their minds?"

"He came to them and said that the spirit of the departed had contacted him and demanded justice. At first the sheriff dismissed Black as a crackpot. But eventually, Black convinced the victim's family to raise enough of a fuss that the coroner took a second look just to shut them up. But he found out that the first one was smothered. Then, with each successive death, it became easier for Black to convince them to check further."

Gloria harrumphed. "But why shouldn't they have immediately —"

Earl cut her off. "So, could Black really do this stuff? This psychic business? I never even heard of him before."

"Yeah, he was a real come-from-out-of-nowhere story. Montague Black sort of burst onto the scene." Page sat forward and counted off on his fingers. "The first death was ruled natural causes; only after Black convinced the sheriff to reopen the investigation did they change the status. The second death was also ruled natural causes; again, Black made the difference. Then this third death —"

"Natural causes?"

"Nope. Black actually called the murder in before it was even discovered."

Earl sat back in his wheelchair. "Now, that sounds suspicious to me."

Page shook his head. "Black had an airtight alibi for each murder. In fact, he was onstage in some club doing his act. There were a hundred witnesses."

Earl scratched his nose. When Montague Black was alive, a hundred witnesses gave him an alibi. When Black was dead, a hundred witnesses fingered his killer.

Gloria urged the other man on. "Then what?"

Page continued. "So this hit the national media, and I smelled a story right away. I flew in and started making friends with all the principles involved."

"Except for Black — he didn't want to

make friends."

"No." Page sat back again, shaking his head. He crossed his legs. "He was working his own angle. This serial killer angle was his brass ring. Once he caught this killer, he was going to have a major national presence. He would be the Oprah of the psychic world. He was getting courted by all sorts of media."

Page clenched a fist and rubbed his fingernails on his shirt. "Black thought my book was a conflict with his plans."

"So he was in your way?"

Page shrugged a shoulder. "I could still get published."

"But without his blessing — or, worse, if he put out some competing story — your book wouldn't go nearly as far."

"Maybe."

"How many sales would you have lost? How much money? How much of your standing in the literary community?"

Page sat on his answer a second. Finally, he said, "I could handle it."

"Then why the argument with Black? Because he was standing in your way. You needed him out of the way."

Page's eyes flared. "Wait — what are you trying to do?"

"No, Mr. Page, what are *you* trying to

do?" Earl grunted. "You had the motive. In all the commotion, you could have slipped into the room there —"

"Stop! I never went in there!" His face was red. Earl glanced over and saw the woman behind the counter stop, too. Page wheezed, "I don't know where you people get off throwing around these crazy accusations. I can do without this." He started to collect his reporter tools.

Earl tilted his head. "That's not a defense, son. If you don't want us to think you're guilty, then maybe you should stop acting guilty."

Page stopped cold. He narrowed his eyes, apparently processing Earl's words. Finally, he spoke. "W–what do you want?"

"Let's say, for the sake of argument, that you are not the murderer." Earl's soft-spoken manner seemed to calm the room. "Then who do you think was? You're a man who researches things for your book. I can't imagine you'd have jumped into this book cold. You would have gathered up some background materials, yes?"

The man's temper seemed to be in check. He let out a big breath. "Yes."

"Who would have a reason to kill Montague Black?"

"Well . . ." Page spoke slowly, measuring

his words. His breathing was tense. "I gathered that as Black's star began to rise, he was ready to dump everyone in his circle."

Earl scratched his nose. "You mean in addition to Ms. Zuniga?"

Page nodded. "Black was also going to dump Carpenter and get a new manager." His eyes stared somewhere. "And I'm not sure what the deal was with that lady at Heritage Care. There seemed like some weird chemistry there."

"Apparently, there was some history there between them."

"Really?" Page lunged for his notepad and pen and began scribbling furiously.

"Well," Earl said, shifting in his wheelchair, "I'm not able to speak on the record. I don't really know much about it."

"That's fine." Scribble, scribble, scribble. Page slapped the notepad shut and looked up, grinning. "All I need is the lead."

Earl tried to get things back on track. "What about all the other folks there in the lobby? Anyone there who might have had a motive?"

Page shrugged. "Time will tell. When you get a room full of crazies together, you don't know what's going to happen. Maybe one of those churchies praying over in the corner got it in their head —"

Gloria cut him off. "Those 'churchies' had no cause to see the man dead. You can be assured of that."

Earl held up a hand and turned to Page. He spoke again in a soft voice. "Montague Black somehow left that room and was either murdered off-site and returned to the room, or he returned and then was murdered."

Page scratched his head. "That's crazy. No one can do that. There were a hundred people outside that room."

"Nonetheless, somehow . . ." Earl held out his hands. "Pastor Benton tells us that when he walked into that room, the room was empty. Montague Black was not in there."

"Really . . ."

"So we're left with two options." Earl held up his left hand. "Either he was lying" — he held up his right hand — "or he was telling the truth."

Page nodded. "And you believe he's telling the truth."

Earl looked the man square in the eye. "Yes. I do."

CHAPTER FIFTEEN

"Pastor Benton is out on bail!" Jenny's voice was entirely too chipper for that time of the morning. Earl had once again stayed up too late reading one of the mystery books Jenny had left on his coffee table — *The Three Coffins* by John Dickson Carr, "locked-room lecture" and all — and he was in no mood for any exuberant phone calls at . . . what time was it? Six in the morning?

"Fine," Earl said, collecting himself. He didn't complain about the time. If it was already six, then daylight was wasting.

"That's all you can say about it? 'Fine'?"

"You said he's out on bail?" Earl shuffled toward the cupboard for a can of coffee. "I don't think you can do that when it's a murder charge."

"Oh, well, maybe they said bond. Whatever it was. The judge ruled that the pastor was not a flight risk. Mr. MacGregor from church put up his property as collateral."

"Wow, that's generous." Earl spooned the coffee grounds into the filter.

"He's not rich, by any means. But the pastor and his family just don't have any property — it all belongs to the church, and the board refused to let him use it to raise bond. So Mr. MacGregor stepped in."

"Uh-huh." Water into the pot. Burner on high. "So where is the pastor now? I guess he can't leave town or anything, right?"

"He's at home with his family. One of the ladies at church tried to put together a welcome home party. I don't think anyone is going to be there."

"When is it?"

"It's today. Anytime today. It's an open house out at the parsonage."

Earl checked the water in the pot. Warm but not boiling yet. He sighed. "So, do we take anything over there?"

"I don't know. I've never been to an open house when someone came home from jail. Usually it's because someone is sick or someone died."

"A party?"

"Well, you know, you bake a casserole or make a salad and take it over so the person doesn't need to cook. I guess Mrs. Benton might be a little too stressed right now to cook. So maybe we should take something.

What should we take?"

"Why are you asking me?" He checked the water and decided it was hot enough. He was too impatient to wait for it to boil. "How about a bucket of chicken?"

"Really? You think so?"

"And some potato salad?"

"I don't know. . . ." Jenny paused on the other end. Her voice dropped to almost a whisper. "Have you talked to Gloria?"

"What, about this? I just now found out about it. You called me, if you remember."

"No, I mean about . . . stuff."

"What stuff?" He poured the water into the sock with the grounds. He set the timer for five minutes.

"You know . . . girlfriend stuff."

Earl felt his ears getting hot. "We don't call it that when you get to my and Gloria's age."

"Well, whatever you call it. You know what I'm asking."

"Yes, I suppose I do. But I don't have anything to report. So what time are we going to the pastor's house today?"

Gloria was off work around lunchtime again. They made plans for her to pick up Earl, and they would head out to visit with the pastor and his family. Jenny would meet them out there.

Gloria and Earl stopped at the grocery store for fried chicken, potato salad, and some fresh fruit. The fruit was Gloria's idea.

"I wonder what kind of mob scene there'll be at the pastor's house?"

Gloria kept her eyes on the road. "You mean the media?"

"No, I mean all the church folk coming and going. Maybe we shouldn't go. I don't want to be an imposition."

"Nonsense! I'm sure the pastor and his wife will appreciate your visiting them. After all, you were a houseguest for almost a month."

"How do you think they're holding up? We've been scrambling so much these past couple days, I didn't even think about how his family might be handling this."

"Well, then it's a good thing we're paying them a visit today."

The pastor's house was next to the church. There were several cars parked along the street and in the church parking lot. There were also a couple of white vans plastered with the brightly colored logos for news organizations.

As Earl got out of the car, he noted that nearly all the cars were occupied. "I guess you were right."

"What?" Gloria was unfolding Earl's wheelchair.

Earl pointed. "The media is veritably swarming."

"Yeah."

They got Earl situated in the wheelchair, the bucket of chicken, container of potato salad, and basket of fresh fruit in his lap. "I feel like one of those vendor carts."

"Hey, it's a living."

They navigated their way through the members of the media. A few heads turned their way, but apparently an old man in a wheelchair with fried chicken, accompanied by an old woman, weren't considered "newsworthy."

They made their way to the door, and Gloria knocked. After a few minutes, the curtain in the nearby window fluttered. Then there was the sound of the door being unlocked.

The door opened, and the pastor's wife, Lanie, was there. She seemed so much older than the last time Earl had seen her. When she noticed Gloria, her eyes brightened. "Gloria! Hello!"

Gloria hugged her. "How are you doing, sweetie?"

"The Lord has us in His hands."

"That's right."

Lanie Benton finally looked down at Earl and smiled. "Earl, I'm glad to see you."

Earl held up the bucket of chicken. "We brought you something."

She accepted the bucket, albeit with a confused expression on her face. "Um, thanks."

"It's fried chicken. We also brought you this potato salad. And the fruit was Gloria's idea."

Loaded down with the perishables, Lanie motioned for them to follow her. "Come in! Come in!"

After Earl and Gloria were across the threshold, he saw the pastor's wife stick her head back out the door then close it and lock it. And dead bolt it. And chain it.

Earl cleared his throat. "So, how is the pastor doing? All things considered?"

"Andy's in the living room if you want to go in."

Gloria patted him on the shoulder. "I'll stay in here and talk with Lanie."

Earl nodded, offering a weak smile to each of them. He put his hands to the rims of his wheels and pushed himself through the house until he got to the living room.

As he went through the familiar hall, memories washed over Earl. He thought back to the events of a few months ago, when he had lost his home at Candlewick Retirement Center. The pastor and his family had opened their home to Earl, a complete stranger. They had shown him the compassion of Christ. It was the first practical expression of the love of Jesus that Earl had ever seen with his own eyes. And he had been the recipient.

As the memories flickered, Earl felt his face warm with shame. To think he had ever doubted the pastor's innocence. How dare the man's own church not give him a total vote of confidence!

Earl reached the living room. It was much the same as when he had stayed with the Bentons: a worn brown and orange couch, a scratched circular coffee table, and shelves and shelves of books. The cream-colored walls were packed with pictures of the family and of the many people they had met and the places they had seen in their travels around the world on mission trips.

The pastor sat on the couch reading, his legs crossed.

Earl hesitated before interrupting. "Pastor Benton?"

When the other man saw him, his face lit up. "Earl! What are you doing here?"

"Oh, um." Earl hesitated, unsure whether the party was supposed to be a surprise.

"Gloria and I just thought we would stop by. With some chicken. And some potato salad."

"Oh. Well, thank you."

"And Gloria brought some fruit." Earl started wringing his hands. "How are you holding up?"

"I won't say it hasn't been difficult." The pastor set the book aside and motioned for Earl to wheel himself closer. "But the Lord is with me every step of the way. Just because I can't see an answer in the natural doesn't mean Jesus isn't working as my advocate in the supernatural."

"Sure." Earl nodded despite the fact he had no idea what the pastor was talking about. He hoped it would come up in the new-members' class at church.

"I've just been rereading some of the passages in the Bible where men of God were unjustly accused — and sometimes even unjustly imprisoned. Joseph in Egypt, Paul in Rome . . . it's comforting to know I'm not alone."

"That's good to hear." Earl made a mental note to look up "Joseph in Egypt" and "Paul in Rome" when he got back home.

"The sovereign Lord is in control, and He's not surprised by any of this." The pastor's mood darkened. "I just feel awful for that poor man. We may not have been friends, but you still hope a man will live long enough to come to salvation."

"A shame."

"And I feel awful for his family, too. I need to see whether I can find them and offer my condolences."

They sat for long moments. Earl heard the hum of the electric clock on the wall. It was a big painting of Jesus with a clock inserted under Him. Under the clock was the inscription, "Jesus saith unto him, I am the way, the truth, and the life: no man cometh unto the Father, but by me. John 14:6."

The silence made Earl nervous. He blurted, "So, have you talked with any of the folks from church?"

He nodded. "The board wants to put my pastorship up for a vote."

"I know. Ouch."

"In the meantime, they're already fielding candidates for possible replacement."

"But how can they do that if you're not even . . . uh . . ." Earl couldn't bring himself to finish the sentence.

"If I'm not even convicted?"

Earl averted his eyes. He whispered, "Yes."

Pastor Benton leaned back, stretching his arms across the couch. "It's important to keep this all in perspective. Do I wish I had a stronger vote of confidence from my congregants? Of course. But they're concerned. And if I were in their place . . . ?"

"You'd railroad them, too?"

Pastor Benton got a twinkle in his eye. "Well, no. But you have to give them some understanding."

Earl shook his head. "I don't know. I guess I'm just having some trouble with all the church politics. This is all new to me."

"Please don't let this stuff sour your view of the church, Earl. Remember, the Church — with the big *C* — is the Body of Christ. We're being made perfect. However, until that day, we're also still the little *c* church, too. And as long as we have human beings for members, we're going to have church politics."

"I'm not thrilled about that."

"You just have to keep your eyes on Christ. He is the Head of the Church."

Earl made a mental note to ask his teacher about it at church.

The pastor asked, "So, how are things going with you and Gloria?"

Earl glanced back over his shoulder. The women were still gabbing in the kitchen. He turned back to the pastor and grinned. "Still working on it. Right after we talked last week, I tried to take her to a nice dinner so we could talk about our relationship."

"And how did that go?"

"Not well."

"I'm sorry, Earl."

"No, I mean, we never had the conversation. Of course, we did have something of a moment yesterday. But I have a hard enough time discussing my feelings as it is, and with all this other stuff going on . . ."

"You shouldn't let my trials get in the way of your own life."

"Well, we've sort of been busy, you know, trying to prove you're innocent. I'm not sure we know what we're doing."

Pastor Benton's eyes lit up. "That was you? I heard someone had been asking around. I assumed it was just another reporter."

"We've been trying to turn over whatever stones we can think of. Not that it has been much help."

"We?"

"Gloria, Jenny Hutton, and me. We were just knocking our heads, trying to come up with an explanation."

"I just appreciate the vote of confidence."

Earl looked at his wrist. No matter how many times he looked, there wasn't a watch on it. "I wonder what's keeping the others."

"Others?"

"Oh, um . . ." Earl still didn't know how much of the open house was to be some kind of surprise. "Jenny was supposed to meet us here. Maybe we'll be able to confer a bit."

"I don't know what else there would be. My lawyer is putting together his case already. It's in the Lord's hands now."

"I just wish we could figure out how a man could disappear in a room like that. What did you see?"

The pastor shrugged. "The room was empty."

"Yes, but what did it look like? The windows, the walls, the fireplace . . ."

"I don't know. . . ."

"You went into the room two times, right? The first time, for your meeting with Black. The second time, after they found the body in there. What was different about the room from the first time to the second time?"

"Well, there were only a couple of minutes between the first time and the second time."

"Exactly. But think back. . . ."

"Okay, the first time . . ." The pastor leaned back, eyes shut tight.

"What did you do? How did you know the room was empty?"

"I walked in, and I looked around. There's

nothing tall enough to stand behind. I looked to see whether there was a door of any kind — a closet or something. The windows were all closed. I looked out the big glass windows, but there didn't seem to be anybody out in the garden. I sat on the couch. There was some kind of gurgling —"

"A what? A 'gurgling'?"

Pastor Benton nodded, eyes still shut. "Yes. From in front of me. It sounded like it was coming from the fireplace."

"Did you do anything to find the source?"

"I went over there, and the grate was closed. Then I stepped on something and looked down to see a letter opener with brown ink on it." He paused, opening his eyes. "I mean, I assumed it was some kind of ink."

"What did you do?"

He let out a defeated sigh. "I picked it up. I assumed Black was trying to play some kind of prank, maybe trying to trick me into looking up the chimney, so he could drop soot or something on me. Big joke." He clucked his tongue. "To think that poor man was dying in there somewhere. . . ."

"So you picked up the letter opener? And, I guess, put it in your pocket?"

The pastor flushed. "Call me an idiot, but that's exactly what I did. It never crossed my mind that Black wasn't trying to pull my leg. I jumped to the conclusion he called all that media out there for the purpose of making me look foolish. And I wasn't going to stand for it."

"So you got out of there before he could pull the trigger on his prank. . . ."

"Yes."

"And gave a hundred witnesses the impression you had just killed a man and were running away with the murder weapon."

Pastor Benton exhaled sadly. "That poor man."

They fell into a silence. Earl considered the pastor's story. "Are you sure the noise came from inside the fireplace?"

He nodded. "It was eerie. So you think the murder took place back behind the fireplace somehow?"

Earl shook his head. "We didn't find any secret passage."

"I assume you checked the blueprints?"

"Um, no."

"Talked with the architect? Maybe took X-ray pictures or did some kind of sonar readings?"

"We banged on all the walls." Earl felt foolish. "I guess we didn't go far enough."

The pastor smiled wearily. "Actually, you've been a great help. And you've given me some ideas. Maybe my lawyer can track down that sort of information."

"Of course, even if there was a secret door . . . how did Montague Black know about it, when nobody else did?"

"A fine question."

"We talked with some of Black's associates, trying to figure out how he'd have pulled that sort of disappearing trick."

"So, he was also a magician?"

"That's just it — he apparently never exhibited any skills as an illusionist. After our talk with Carpenter, Jenny got on the computer and we looked up Black's record. He wasn't an escape artist, he didn't do card tricks, none of it. In fact, before this whole serial killer business even started, Montague Black was just doing some club act as a mentalist. You know, the assistant goes out into the audience and gets the information, which is then secretly fed to the man onstage."

The pastor nodded. "Sadly, I've seen con artists pretending to be men of God use the same sorts of tricks. The so-called prophet is up onstage, and the helpers are out in the audience. I've seen them use code words, sometimes some kind of setup with a microphone and earphone. Or some charlatans are simply great at reading people."

"I think you said something there, pastor."
"What?"
Earl turned toward the kitchen. "Gloria!"
She rushed into the living room. "What is it?"
"Montague Black was an expert at reading people."
She blinked at him. "Okay . . ."
"So how did he 'read' complete strangers who were already dead?"

Chapter Sixteen

They called Jenny and told her to meet them at the library instead of the pastor's house, quickly said their goodbyes to the Bentons, and Gloria got Earl into the car. Once she was in the driver's seat, she snapped her seat belt and adjusted her rear-view mirror. "Now what?"

"We've been mixing different kinds of things together. Montague Black was a mentalist — not a sorcerer, not a conjurer, not any of that. He wasn't anything that didn't involve somehow tricking people into thinking he knew what was on their mind."

"Does it make any difference?"

"Whether you look at this guy from a *natural* standpoint or from a *supernatural* standpoint, he never had the ability to disappear from a room or reappear in a room."

"Okay. I feel like we've been through this."

"Not only have we been mixing up a bunch of different skill sets, we've also missed a major difference between how Black was operating his scam and how that suddenly changed shortly before his death."

"I'm sorry. You're talking in circles here."

Earl took a deep breath. "Montague Black was working as a mentalist — a stage act. Then a few weeks ago, he suddenly sprouts the ability to know whether a complete stranger was murdered? That's spontaneous information. It has nothing to do with *'cold reading'* people, nothing to do with a hidden microphone."

She considered this. "He claimed to be in touch with the spirits."

"Right, but for most of his career, being 'in touch with the spirits' meant he could tell you your birthday or whether his assistant was holding your car keys or your watch — and then one day he starts solving crimes? No, there's a discrepancy — he was suddenly working on a whole scale he had never worked on before. Ever."

"It seems mighty slim."

"It's all we have. And, frankly, it's a lead I bet the FBI never thought to pursue. I mean, what's the link with the three victims? What's the common denominator?"

"Don't you think the FBI is pursuing that now? They have national databases, they have resources, they have computers, and —"

"No matter how many ways they look at the victims, I bet they missed the one thing they had in common."

"And that would be . . . ?"

"Montague Black. He's the common denominator."

"But he had an alibi each time."

"Black was hitching his wagon to this serial killer — national media attention, a television contract, maybe a book. This serial killer was his ticket. He had to get his information from somewhere."

Earl waited for Gloria to process all this. She stared out the windshield, gripping the steering wheel tightly. "You think he could have overheard the killer talking about it somewhere?"

Earl grunted. "Once, maybe. But three times?"

"Maybe he had some inside track with the police. They know the identity of the killer but for some reason passed that information —"

Earl rubbed his hands together. "If Sheriff Meyer knew the identity of the serial killer, don't you think he'd pass it along to the feds just to get them off his back?"

"Maybe . . ."

"And if the deputy had helped Black pretend he was psychic, do you really think he'd still be running around trying to prove the man levitated out of the room?"

"I suppose not."

Earl set his jaw, thinking. "I guess we could say the same about any of those reporters. If they knew the identity of the serial killer, wouldn't it make more sense to simply turn the killer in and get the exclusive?"

"I don't know what to think anymore." Gloria started the car and turned on the heater. She started to shift into DRIVE but stopped. "So, what does any of this prove?"

Earl rubbed his chin. "If we expect to solve the murder of Montague Black, we have to figure out the identity of the Mercy Killer."

At the library, Jenny scrunched up her face at Earl. "Why are we here? Don't get me wrong — I'm glad you're finally at the library."

Gloria put a hand on Jenny's arm. "Earl had an idea, and we had to come here to pursue it."

Earl said, "We've been going about this all wrong. We need to investigate the victims of the serial killer."

Jenny wrinkled her nose. "But they don't even know if there is a serial killer."

Earl waved that away. "That's irrelevant to my point."

"Which is . . . ?"

Gloria and Earl explained his theory and how Black tied it all together. Jenny furrowed her brow, nodding thoughtfully. "But if these murders are the work of some crazy person, there's some random thought process at work, isn't there?"

Earl nodded. "Maybe. Although one of your detectives said something along the lines of even crazy people work by their own logic — the trick is to figure that pattern out."

"One of my detectives? You read one of the books I left you?"

"I may have read one. Or two. Anyway, Montague Black was somehow involved in those deaths."

"What if he made the whole thing up? Maybe these people died of natural causes, and he came in after the fact and lied about it."

Earl tapped his index finger to his lips, thinking. "No. The police investigated each death and determined they were murders. His death was related — maybe he was murdered for what he knew."

Jenny took them to the computer and looked up the names of the three victims: Rebecca Vollman, Victor Caddigan, and Cloris Thomas. She found all three obituaries, plus recent news stories that mentioned any or all of the names. As she printed each new article out, Earl skimmed the pages. He noted what the three deaths had in common:

1. At first glance, all three deaths were or would have been chalked up to natural causes.
2. Upon an alert from Montague Black, the first two deaths were reopened and discovered to have been murder. The third death was reported by Black as a murder before anyone had even found the body.
3. When the coroner reexamined the three bodies, he was able to determine that all three were suffocated with a pillow.
4. All three victims were elderly.

The first victim, Rebecca Vollman, was a resident of Watson Retirement Home, in nearby Burgoon. The second victim, Victor Caddigan, apparently lived alone at home. The third victim, Cloris Thomas, was a resident at Heritage Care.

Earl read the printouts again. And again.

There was nothing in these stories to indicate any of the victims were dying or terminally ill. There was no valid reason indicated for referring to these deaths as "merciful."

"There's so little to link these three people together. They didn't live in the same area. Two of them are women, and one is a man. Two of them lived in an assisted-care facility; one of them lived at home." He set the papers on the table. "There should be more than that."

Jenny frowned. "Like what?"

"It's like in that book — even a crazy person is following some kind of pattern, even if it only makes sense to him." Earl rubbed his forehead. "Maybe the newspapers are withholding certain facts at the request of the authorities. Or maybe the authorities have found something that hasn't been released to the press."

Jenny laughed uneasily. "But what does any of this matter? This is a federal investigation you're talking about. You can't meddle in this."

"Don't you understand? If we want to find the answer to *our* question, we have to first figure out the answer to *this* question." He tapped the papers on the table.

"They won't see it that way. Before, you were just some crazy old man sniffing around a case that was closed. Now you're going to be a crazy old man getting tangled up in an ongoing federal investigation. That's going to be a problem."

Earl rubbed his hands. "Think about Pastor Benton. If we ever expect to get him off the hook, we need to find this serial killer."

"But if the FBI is on this case, then they're going to solve it. That's what they do. They have enormous resources at their disposal."

Gloria said, "Earl thinks they're looking in the wrong place."

"He can't know that."

Earl pointed a bony finger toward the banks of computer terminals across the way. "How can we contact the families and friends of the victims?"

"I–I'm not sure." She bit her lip. "If I were some kind of hacker stalker or something, I could probably find you their social security numbers. But if all I have . . ."

"The obituaries mentioned names of relatives." Earl reached for the stack of papers then stopped. "Of course, even with the names, we could call the wrong people. There's something awkward about calling someone to ask whether they have a relative who was murdered."

Jenny agreed. "There's no smooth transition out of that."

Earl asked, "What about asking Deputy Fisher? He'd have the exact information we need."

"I don't know. . . ." Jenny blushed. "Why would he tell us?"

"You two are dating, aren't you?"

"We're not dating."

"Whatever you kids call it. You're sweet on each other."

"After the past few days, I don't think he's very sweet on me."

Gloria said, "You'd be surprised."

"Just call him," Earl requested.

"Maybe this isn't the best time. He's on duty."

"Fine. No reason to bait him unnecessarily." Earl looked at his wrist. He really needed to get a watch. "The day is getting away from us."

Gloria asked, "What can we do?"

Earl smiled. "I know who we can call — Hamilton Page, true-crime writer."

Chapter Seventeen

Gloria said, “You must be joking.”

Earl held out his hands. “Why?”

“I don’t trust that man. Besides, he’s one of your suspects.”

Jenny wrinkled her nose. “Who are you talking about?”

Earl recounted his and Gloria’s meeting with Page. He turned his attention back to Gloria. “He’s done all the research on this case already. He’s either tracked down all the families and spoken with them by now, or he will soon. Why not save ourselves the trouble of treading over the same ground?”

Jenny looked at Gloria. “I hate to say it, but he’s making sense.”

Gloria said, “But he already refused to help us.”

“Yeah, but we were working on a different murder then.” He reached out. “Give me his card. It can’t hurt to call.”

Gloria hesitated, her face a mask of frustration. Finally, she grudgingly dug through her purse and handed him the man's business card. "I don't like this. Not one bit."

"What's the harm?"

"He could turn out to be the killer. He could murder all of us."

Earl hesitated, the card in his hand. Finally, he shook off the thought and handed the card to Jenny. "Call the number there."

"Why me?"

"You're the one with the cellular telephone."

She handed him the phone. "And now you have it."

Accepting the phone, he grimaced at her. Then he squinted at the number on the card. It took him some fumbling to punch the tiny buttons in the correct combination. He put the phone up to his ear. "It's ringing. Hello? Mr. Hamilton Page? This is Earl Walker. We met at the —"

"I remember you," the voice on the other end said. "What do you want?"

"We were hoping you could help us with some research."

"You gotta be kidding me. You accuse me of murder, and now you expect me to help you prove it? If you want to get your guilty preacher off the hook, you have to come up with a different fall guy."

Earl forced himself to chuckle, hoping it made him sound friendly. "Actually, this is about something else. We need your help getting in contact with the relatives of the victims of the Mer — of the serial killer."

There was a pause on the other end. Earl glanced up at Gloria. Her disapproving frown was replaced with one of concern. He winked at her.

The man asked, "Why are you doing that?"

"We reached a dead end, so we're looking for a new path. Given the topic of your book, we assume you've already done a lot of the research. . . ."

"That's right, I've done the work already. Why should I share it with you? You might try to beat me to market."

"I can assure you, Mr. Page, writing a book is the furthest thing from my mind." Earl hesitated. "Besides, I can't imagine attempting to match the level of your prose."

There was a pause on the other end. "So you have some legitimate lead?"

"Yes."

"Well . . ." There was another pause. "I suppose even if you fall on your face, it could still make an interesting subplot."

"What?"

"Fine. It's agreed."

"Wait, what's agreed?"

"I'll give you the research you need, and I get the exclusive rights to your story."

"Oh. I'm not sure whether I —"

"If you stumble across something useful, I'll be right there to record it. And when the FBI throws you in prison for obstruction of justice, I'll record that, too. Either way, I get something exclusive."

Earl breathed through his nose. "That's not exactly what I had in mind."

"It's the only way I'll do it. I share my notes with you, and you give me an exclusive. Take it or leave it."

Earl put the phone on his chest. "He wants to make fools of us."

Jenny asked, "So he's not going to help at all?"

"Oh, he'll help us. He'll help us all the way to federal prison." Earl took a deep breath. He said into the phone, "Agreed. But I need to speak to these people personally."

"But I've already interviewed most of —"

"That's the only way I'll do it. Take it or leave it."

Page agreed and made arrangements to pick Earl up in the morning. Earl asked whether Page had photographs of four specific people whom Earl named — which he did — and Earl stressed that Page needed to bring those photos with him to the interviews. When the conversation was finished, Earl closed the phone and handed it to Jenny, who put it back in her purse.

Gloria asked, "Are you crazy?"

Earl set his jaw. "Do you believe that Pastor Benton is innocent or not?"

She stared back at him. Her mouth worked, but no words came out.

The trunk of Page's rental car was too small for Earl's wheelchair, so they piled into Gloria's car. Gloria was clearly unhappy with the arrangement but said nothing. Despite the protests of both men, she and Jenny had insisted on meeting the men at Earl's house and tagging along to protect him.

The first stop was to meet Colleen Ferguson, daughter of Rebecca Vollman. Page said she would be coming to the end of her school day — she was a first grade teacher — and they could speak with her as she headed to her car.

Gloria asked, "Why don't we give her the courtesy of letting her go home first?"

Page shook his head. "If we speak to her outside, she won't feel like somebody is listening. Besides, if we can get to her before she gets home to her kids or her husband, she's more likely to be frank with us."

Earl raised an eyebrow. "So, rudeness leads to frankness."

"You'd be surprised."

They reached the school and, despite Gloria's protests, parked in the teacher's lot. Nobody spoke as they waited. Earl checked his wrist. He really needed to get a watch.

Finally, there was a bell. Earl discovered if he tilted his head far enough, he could peek around the side of the school and see the children spilling out. Most of them headed either for the school buses or for the cars of waiting adults.

Another block of time passed, and some grown-ups began exiting out the back of the school, in ones and twos. Page watched closely. Finally, he sat up. "There." He opened the driver side door, glancing back. "Come on!"

"I need my wheelchair!"

Gloria put a hand on Earl's shoulder. "I'll get it."

While Page rocketed off to catch Mrs. Ferguson, Gloria went to the trunk and got out Earl's wheelchair. She unfolded it. She brought it around to his passenger door.

She helped Earl into it. Until now, it had never occurred to him what a lengthy ordeal this process was.

Once he was in the wheelchair, Earl put his hands to the rims of his wheels and started to push forward. He barely got started when he saw that Page and the young woman were actually coming in his direction. He stopped, Gloria and Jenny on either side of him.

As the young lady drew close, Earl saw she was an attractive brunette, probably in her late fifties, her hair pulled back in a bun. Her demeanor was marred by the weariness carved on her face.

Page made the introductions. "This is Mrs. Colleen Ferguson, the daughter of Rebecca Vollman. This is Earl Walker. He's a special investigator on your mother's case."

The woman's interest seemed piqued. She sniffled and wiped an eye. "Really? But I thought the FBI was already working on this case."

Earl felt awkward. He didn't want to risk somehow exploiting this woman's pain. "We're here to help them."

"But I already went through all this with the sheriff and then again with the FBI." She glanced at Page. "And you already interviewed me on tape. Do I really have to go through all that again? I'm not sure I have the strength."

Earl held up a hand. "We don't want to keep you long, Mrs. Ferguson. Just a few questions."

She nodded tentatively. "O–okay."

Earl held out his hand to Page. "Give me the photographs." Page ran to the car then came back and handed Earl a camera. Earl grunted, "What am I supposed to do with this?"

"You can preview the pictures here." Page pressed a few buttons. A picture came up of Montague Black, a candid shot taken outside Heritage Care.

Earl held out the camera to Mrs. Ferguson. "Do you recognize this man?"

Wiping a hand across her nose, she nodded slowly. "I saw him on television. It's that psychic man, isn't it?"

"Other than the television, have you ever seen or spoken with him?" Mrs. Ferguson shook her head. Earl continued, "How about your mother? Had she said anything about him? Would she have known about him for any reason?"

"Not that I know of."

"How about . . ." Earl had Page advance the photos until it got to a picture of Divina Zuniga, speaking with her cameraman at the scene of the meeting. "How about this woman? Did you or your mother ever see or hear of this woman? Divina Zuniga? She's a television producer."

The response was also negative. They showed her a digital photograph of manager Jack Carpenter and one of activities director Sheree Jackson. Each time, the response was negative. Neither Mrs. Ferguson nor, so far as she knew, her mother had ever seen or heard of any of these people before.

"How about this man?" He pointed to Page, who was clearly surprised to be pointed at in such a manner. "Did you know anything about this man prior to your mother's death? Or had she?"

The answer was negative.

"When you spoke to the authorities, did any of them show you photographs of these five people?"

The answer was again negative.

"I see." Earl thought for a second. "Did your mother have any kind of illness?"

"She was sickly, if that's what you mean. But nothing serious."

"There was no specific reason to worry about her health?"

"No. We just thought she had died in her sleep. We were already making the funeral arrangements when we got the awful call that . . . that . . ."

"I understand." Earl paused, careful to be sensitive to her feelings. "I imagine you read about the others who were, um . . ." The woman nodded. Earl moved on. "Was there anything in any of the reports that seemed unusual to you?"

The woman wrinkled her brow. "Like what?"

"Like some connection between your mother and the others? Had you seen or heard of any of them before?"

"No. Do we have to keep talking about this? It sounds like just some random crazy person killed them."

Earl chose not to share Hercule Poirot's theory about crazy serial killers and their private patterns. Instead, he thanked the woman for her time and let her go home.

As the rest of them headed back to Gloria's car, Page threw a fit. "That's it? You show a few pictures and just ask a couple of questions? Why couldn't you have just sent me back to her? We didn't need all four of us to do that — I could have done it myself."

"Not exactly."

Page stopped the parade. "Why? What did you get?"

Earl pursed his lips, puffing his cheeks. "I'll tell you when I know."

"Remember, you promised me an exclusive."

"Don't worry." Earl smiled. "You'll get everything that's coming to you."

They drove out to the Caddigans'. Pete Caddigan was the grandson of Victor Caddigan, the second victim of the so-called "Mercy Killer."

Reaching his house, they were met by the man's wife and what sounded like a horde of screaming children bouncing off the walls. Mrs. Caddigan wore an apron, and she wiped her hands on a kitchen towel. Pete was working late at the office, she said, but was expected home after six. "You're welcome to wait for him if you like."

Page said, "Sure!"

Earl winced at a child's squeal. "Thank you."

The woman showed the four to the living room. Gloria and Jenny sat on the couch. Page took the edge of the recliner. Earl, after some difficulty getting the wheelchair over the threshold, parked next to the lamp in the corner.

They waited a grueling forty minutes, regularly accosted by overstimulated moppets. Every time the adults in the room tried to begin any kind of conversation, no matter how inconsequential, some child would bound in and launch into an impromptu session of show-and-tell.

If nothing else, Earl saw the wisdom of ambushing Mrs. Ferguson out in the parking lot at her place of work. If only they had done the same for Mr. Caddigan.

More than once Earl tried to ask Page why they hadn't done just that, but every time Earl started a sentence there was some new interruption. Finally he just gave up and waited. He regularly looked at his wrist. He really needed to get a watch.

From his vantage point, he could barely peek through the curtain at the boring suburban tracts across the street. Finally, he saw a car pull into the driveway.

There was the sound of the garage door opening and the car rumbling its way in. Around the corner of the living room, Earl could hear a door open. If he had any question about the identity of the person entering, it was answered by a chorus of tiny voices shrieking, "Daddy! Daddy! Daddy!"

Even Mrs. Caddigan made an appearance, coming from the kitchen to greet her husband. She kissed him lightly on the cheek then motioned that he had guests waiting in the living room. They spoke in low tones.

Finally, he came into the room. "What do

you want here?"

Page stood and offered a hand. "Hello again, sir, I'm —"

"I remember you. I asked you a question."

"Oh." Page rubbed the back of his neck with one hand and motioned toward them with the other. "These folks are here to just ask a few questions. We won't take much of your time."

"What questions? Haven't I told you people enough?"

"Well, these are special investigators —"

"I've already given my statement to the authorities. If that's not good enough, they'll have to ask me the rest of them in a court of law." He whirled and headed out of the room. At the door to the hall he passed Mrs. Caddigan, nervously wiping her hands with the kitchen towel. He barked, "Get rid of them."

She came in apologetically. "He had a hard day at the office. You understand."

"Yes," Earl said, although he didn't. "Maybe you could help us, Mrs. Caddigan. We just want you to look at a couple of photographs —"

The man appeared again, his office shirt unbuttoned and tie dangling around his neck. "Why are you here? My grandfather died of natural causes! Get out!"

■ ■ ■ ■

The next of kin for Cloris Thomas was a cousin named Cole MacDonald. Page had no idea how to stage one of his *"ambushes"* this time, so he made an appointment to come see him that night.

"It's just as well," Earl said. "If this past visit is an example of your ambush journalism, you can have it."

Page laughed. "You take the good and the bad. Not everyone wants to talk. Sometimes not even because they're guilty."

Finding the address given by MacDonald, they ended up at a dingy motel in the town of Dyersfield. The parking lot was empty, scant light offered by the flickering lamps along the concrete.

Doors dotted the circumference of each floor, each room with its own individual outside door. Mr. MacDonald's room was apparently on the second floor, only accessible by the outdoor stairs.

"I guess I'll have to show him the pictures myself," Page said.

"No. He needs to come down here."

"I'll just get your questions answered, and I'll be right back."

"Okay — deal's off." Earl craned his neck

to the backseat. "Gloria, do you wanna go ahead and drive me home? We're done with Mr. Page here." She nodded and opened her passenger door.

"Wait!" Page held out his hands. He paused then let out a big sigh. "Fine. I'll ask him to come down and speak with you." He left them, muttering to himself.

Jenny leaned forward in her seat. "They probably have an elevator, Mr. Walker. We would just have to —"

"We're fine here."

After some minutes, Page and another man reached the car. "This is Earl Walker. Earl, this is Cole MacDonald." In the dim parking lot lighting, Earl saw a gaunt man who looked to be a little younger than himself.

Earl's window down, he shook the man's hand. "Good to meet you. I want to express my condolences for your loss."

The man waved it off. "Thank you, but as I told this gentleman yesterday, I didn't really know my cousin well. I'm just out here to wrap up some final details with her estate."

"Oh. Well, just the same, we appreciate your willingness to help."

"What did you need?"

Earl motioned for the camera. Page

showed MacDonald the digital photos of Jack Carpenter, Sheree Jackson, Divina Zuniga, and Montague Black.

No, he had never seen nor heard of any of them prior to the death of his cousin. Neither had he seen nor heard of Hamilton Page prior to that. He had no way of knowing whether his cousin had seen any of them or not. He had no idea whether his cousin had any serious illness.

"I'm sorry," the man said. "I know it sounds terrible, but I never got to know my cousin. We just lived such different lives."

"How did you end up with her estate?"

"I'm the last living relative they could find. To be frank, I didn't even know she lived out here in Noelton."

"Where did you think she was?"

The man shrugged. "I never thought about it."

Chapter Eighteen

In the car, Earl said, "Well, that was useless. The families didn't know these people at all. For most of 'em, an old person's just another disposable toaster to throw in the back of the closet and forget."

In the back, Page scribbled furiously. Gloria turned and glowered. "What are you writing? Did you get something useful?"

Page looked up with a grin, pointing his eraser toward Earl. "I'm writing this down. Your whole failed investigation will make a great angle for the book!"

Earl glared. "Don't write this down! This is not for the book!"

Page was back to his scribbling, mumbling to himself as he went, "Walker was . . . humiliated . . . and didn't want . . . anyone . . . to know it."

"Why are you writing about me? Stop that!"

"He . . . asked me . . . to stop writing. . . ."

When Earl grabbed at the notebook, Page yanked it out of reach. He grinned anew and went back to his scribbling. At least he stopped mumbling his notes aloud as he wrote them.

Earl turned back to face the front. "Let's get out of here."

Gloria started the car and drove out of the lot. "Where to now? Do we just go home?"

"I guess." Earl put his hand to the side of his face and stared out his window. He kept vacillating between confidence and doubt. Could he figure this thing out? Should he give up?

As if she read his mind, Jenny reached and squeezed his shoulder. "Don't worry, Mr. Walker. I believe in you."

He shook his head, watching the street-lights flash their way past the car. "If this were one of your detective stories, we'd have already found the killer. But we're just running around in circles. On the other hand, I can't shake the nagging feeling. . . ."

Page stopped scribbling.

Gloria asked, "What?"

Earl was startled out of his reverie. "I was just thinking."

Everyone in the car waited. Finally, Jenny asked, "Yes . . . ?"

"We've been talking to the wrong people. We need to go where these people lived and talk to their friends and neighbors."

Page mumbled, "Uh-huh," and went back to his notebook. It was really starting to bug Earl, but he had nothing to say about it.

Gloria asked, "So we need to find those people tonight?"

Earl looked out at the streetlights as they passed. It was getting dark. "No, it would be too late."

Page said, "Aw, c'mon, it's still early!"

"Not if you're going to interview a bunch of retirees."

"Oh. Right." Scribble, scribble, scribble. "So the plan would be . . . ?"

"We talk to them tomorrow." Earl turned to Gloria. "What's your schedule like? Can you give me a ride?"

"I work all day. And don't forget, tomorrow night is the church board meeting."

Page said, "I can take you."

Earl turned to Jenny in back. "How about you? Can you give me a ride?"

"I have to be at school tomorrow. I've got a big test."

Earl sighed. "Well, I guess that means tomorrow is off."

Page said, "I can take you."

After a pause, Earl grumbled, "Fine."

Gloria shot Earl a nervous glance. They didn't talk the rest of the way.

They dropped off Jenny and wished her a good night. "See you at church tomorrow night," she said. "Don't forget!"

Back at Earl's apartment, Page got into his car and left.

Gloria was silent as she pulled out the wheelchair and helped Earl into the chair. She let him wheel himself to the door.

Earl said, "I guess I won't see you until tomorrow night?"

"If at all." She folded her arms as if the air were chilly. It wasn't.

"What's that supposed to mean?"

"I can't believe you're going to go gallivanting off with that man."

"We'll hardly be gallivanting." Earl put a hand on his leg. "I can't do much of that anymore."

"You know what I mean. Hamilton Page could be a cold-blooded killer, and you'll be alone with him."

"He's the one with all the research, remember? He knows how to open doors and talk to people. Besides, I can handle myself okay."

"Have you noticed how big he is? I bet he's really strong. And those tattoos . . . he looks like he was in the navy or prison or something."

"Hey. Come on now. Everything is going to be fine. The Lord is with us. 'Greater is he that is in you, than he that is in the world.' "

Gloria wiped a tear from her eye. At that moment, Earl never wanted more to propose to her. But it was hardly the time.

Earl barely slept that night. He got up early in the morning and started reading the Bible and praying. This was all still fairly new for him, but he knew he needed to rely on the Lord now more than ever.

This wasn't one of Jenny's detective mysteries, where the victim died bloodlessly over tea and crumpets. This was serious. One or more people had committed several very real, very violent murders.

At eight o'clock, Hamilton Page showed up at Earl's door with coffee and bagels. Earl had to decline the bagel — the bread was too hard for his dentures — but he welcomed the coffee. He'd been so engrossed in his Bible and prayer that he forgot to make any.

Page sat at the table. Mouth full of bagel, he said, "I figured we'd head out to Watson Retirement Home in Burgoon." Swallow. "That's where Rebecca Vollman bought it."

Horrified by the man's casual attitude, Earl started to second-guess this arrangement. But he reminded himself that he didn't trust the man to do this without him, especially given the chance — contrary to what he had told Gloria — Page might turn out to be covering for his own crimes.

Page took another bite of his bagel and, chewing, continued. "Then we'll swing by the home of Victor Caddigan." He waved the half-eaten bagel to emphasize his words. "We'll look around, see who we can find."

"Uh-huh."

"And then we'll drive out to Heritage Care. That's where Cloris Thomas lived. Same drill there."

"I assume you've called ahead to make some kind of appointments."

Page stopped chewing. "Who would I call?"

"Well, the . . . um . . ." Earl stopped. He waved his hand. "Fine. Do what you like. As long as we're done in time for church."

"Aw, you can go to church anytime."

Earl shook his head. "Tonight is a business meeting at church. The board wants to take a vote on whether to keep Pastor Benton."

"Whether to keep . . ." Page scrambled for his notebook and pencil and began writing furiously. "This is great! Can anyone come to this meeting?"

"You have to be a member to vote. But I guess anyone can come watch."

"This is great! Now all we need is a love story."

Earl sat up. "For what?"

"For this book. So far, it has murder, politics, intrigue, the whole ESP angle. . . . If we can get a love story in there, we've got gold!" He pointed the eraser end at Earl. "I don't suppose . . . ?"

Earl eyed the other man suspiciously "You don't suppose what?"

"I don't suppose that college girl is in love with the preacher or anything, is she?"

"He's a married man!"

Page waved it off. "No matter. We'll find a romantic angle somewhere."

Naturally, Earl thought of Gloria. But he wasn't about to share that with this man.

When they went out to Page's rental car, it took some doing for Page to get Earl's wheelchair folded up and in the backseat. He tried to make a case for leaving the wheelchair behind, but Earl wouldn't have it. If Hamilton Page did turn out to be the killer, Earl couldn't defend himself as a lame man without his wheels.

Page checked his notes for directions

before driving off. Eyes on the road, he asked, "So, what's your story?"

"Eh? What story is that?"

"You know. What were you before you were . . . well, you know."

"Before I was what? Widowed? Retired? Old?"

"Uh . . ."

"When I was important, I was a metro bus driver. Is that what you're asking?"

"Sure." Page squinted at a street sign, consulted his notes, then turned his eyes back to the road. "How long did you do that?"

"I was a bus driver for twenty-five years. There was an incident, I lost the use of my legs, and I was forced into retirement." Earl clicked his dentures. "I've been in a wheelchair ever since."

"So what happened?"

"Well, I spent a lot of time at home, underfoot, until my wife died —"

"No, on the bus."

"What do you mean? I drove the route in the —"

"You said there was an 'incident'. . . ."

Earl stared out the passenger window, counting the trees as they passed. "I don't want to talk about it."

"Oh no. You're not going to leave me

hanging. You don't just start a story and then not tell what happened."

"I didn't 'start' a story. You brought it up."

"How could I bring it up? I didn't know anything about it." Page glanced at his notes and made a turn into a parking lot. The sign announced WATSON RETIREMENT HOME.

Earl grunted. "Here we are! Let's catch us a killer!"

"Don't change the subject."

"Who's changing the subject?"

The journalist gathered up his tools. "I'll get to you soon enough."

Earl ignored the threat and clapped his hands together. "So, have you talked to any of these people before?"

"I tried, but they weren't very forthcoming. But maybe if someone of their generation were to talk to them . . . ?"

"Glad to be your token old person," Earl grumbled, privately glad he had an edge. Page wrestled the wheelchair out of the backseat, taking the time to curse the stain it left on the seat. Finally, he got Earl situated in the chair.

Inside, they found a young woman behind the desk. Page allowed Earl to take the lead. Earl felt a little shaky about it but refused to let it show. "Hello! We're here to see Rebecca Vollman's room. We understand that she lived here?"

The woman at the desk rolled her eyes. "They've already come and gone."

Earl and Page exchanged a glance. Earl looked at the woman, leaning forward. "Who's already gone?"

"The FBI." The woman took an emery board to her nails. "They took all the records, the furniture, everything."

"Yes, but we're independent investigators. All we need to see is the room."

The woman looked at Earl. "Who are you, Ironside?"

Earl frowned. "How do you know about Ironside?"

"They invented this thing called the *'rerun'.*"

"Of course."

"So . . . you're a private eye or something?"

Earl grunted. "Or something."

The woman stopped filing her nails long enough to give them directions. When the men got to the room, they found it cleaned out. No chairs, no desk, even the mattress was gone, leaving the bed's empty frame. If there had been anything on the walls or on the linoleum floor, it was all gone now.

Page stepped into the room and whirled around in disbelief. "I can't believe it. Why would they take everything?"

Earl looked around in the hall. "I'm not here to see the room — the feds don't need my help with the evidence."

"Evidence is always important. I remember one time —"

"I don't doubt that evidence is important. But the police and the FBI have resources available to them that we can't even hope to match. They've got all those computers, and their databases, all the microscopes and such, not to mention all the manpower. . . ."

"If you're so down on us, why did you drag me out here?"

Earl let a smile curve his lips. "You didn't let me finish."

Page waved his hand. "By all means, go ahead."

"If there is some piece of evidence here that could make the difference — a fingerprint, a strand of hair, what have you — we can be sure that it's been found and taken to a lab somewhere. I'm not here for the room." Earl held up a finger. "I'm here to meet the neighbors." He put his hands to the rims of his wheels. He went to the next door down the hall and knocked.

A voice behind him called out, "He's probably down in the TV room."

Earl had to turn his chair around to see

the speaker, an older woman wearing a purplish dress with blue flowers. He thumbed toward the empty room. "Did you know Ms. Vollman?"

The woman nodded. "We used to knit together. You want to see?"

Before Earl could stop her, the woman disappeared into a room. After a few seconds, she appeared again, holding a large, half-finished afghan.

"Becky was working on this."

"May I see it?"

Earl took the woven yarn in his hands. It was lovingly crafted, with interlocking patterns of yellows and greens and blues. He didn't imagine it held any kind of clue, but there was something about holding an item that had belonged to Rebecca Vollman that made her seem more like a real person.

He handed it back. "It's very nice."

The woman smiled, holding the afghan close. "Ain't it?"

"So you were friends with Ms. Vollman?"

The woman nodded, her eyes welling up.

Earl glanced over at Page, who had his notebook and pencil in hand then turned back to the woman. "Tell me, did she have any kind of illness?"

She thought for a second then shook her head. "Not that I know of."

"Was she depressed? Any kind of trouble?"
"Not that she said."
"Would she have told you?"
The woman held up the afghan. "We knitted together."
Earl turned to Page. "Pictures."
The man jumped for his digital camera, flipping through the gadget's memory until he found the series of photos Earl wanted. Page put the screen in front of the woman and pointed where to look. She didn't recognize any of the faces — at first.
"Wait, back up there. No, not that one. Not that — there!" She pointed. Page pulled the camera back to keep her from touching the screen. She nodded. "Yeah, that one's familiar."
Page showed Earl the picture of Montague Black. Earl asked, "Did you see him on TV or something?"
"Oh sure. And then there was that time."
Earl and Page exchanged a look. Page asked, "What time?"
"Why, he was at the community center. I think he did some kind of spoon trick or something." She put her hands on her hips. "Let me think now. . . . Yes, he pulled some folks out of their chairs and told them all about themselves." The woman put a hand

on her chest. "Of course, you know it's all a trick."

"Of course. Did Ms. Vollman also see him there?"

The woman seemed amazed that Earl had to ask. "We all went there."

"When was that?"

"Oh, I don't know. They have a different guest every Wednesday. That fella was not quite my cup of tea. But there was this horse act — now that was something!"

"I'm sure it was. But if you could just —"

"The man would ask someone in the audience to think of a number, and the horse would read his mind and tap its hoof on the floor to tell that exact number! Can you imagine that?"

"Um, sure, but —"

"How a horse can read your mind, I'll never know. You can't fake something like that."

Earl couldn't figure out how to politely get her to stop. "Of course."

"Oh, and then there was the guy with the plates!"

Hamilton Page started packing up to go.

"He'd juggle 'em," she continued, "and then he'd put them on these sticks. . . ."

"Well, thank you for your time," Earl said,

not sure she heard him. "You've been very —"

"Of course, his hands were kinda shaky, so the plates kept falling."

Earl gave up trying to find a polite exit. "We, uh . . . have to go."

"Oh, and then the time we saw the parrot."

"Uh-huh." Earl wheeled himself away slowly, as nonchalantly as he could.

"It could sing any song you named."

"Mm-hmm."

"In Korean."

Somehow, Earl and Page extricated themselves and found their way back to the lobby. Page said, "So, do we circle around and go in the back way?"

"For what?"

"She said the other neighbor was in the TV room. That must be around somewhere back in the —"

"We have what we need. Let's go to the next place on the list."

Back at Heritage Care again — Earl was getting sick of this place — they found a group of seniors playing cards out under a big umbrella.

"Cloris? Sure, we knew her." The woman, careful to shield her cards from the man next to her, set a card down on the table. "What do you want to know?"

"Wait a second," the man across from her said. "Why are you fellas asking? Do y'all have IDs?"

Earl coughed into his fist. "No, sir. We're not —"

The man squinted at Page. "Hey! You were here before! We told you to scram!"

Page tried unsuccessfully to hide behind Earl, while Earl tried to placate the man. "Sir, we're just here to find the truth. Don't you want whoever killed your friend to be brought to justice?"

"Hmph." The third person at the table, a man in a blue tractor cap, threw his cards down. Apparently he was out of the game. "What does justice have to do with it? Where were you when Clo was murdered?"

Earl was taken aback. "W–what?"

"What's the use now? It's too late to save her."

Earl looked at Page. The other man looked back with an expression that said, *See what I mean?* Earl looked back at the table, avoiding eye contact with the angry man. He appealed to the other three, all of whom were focused on their cards. "I sympathize with your sorrow."

"Ha!" The angry man crossed his legs,

folding his arms.

"Did any of you know whether Ms. Thomas suffered any sort of illness?"

The woman looked up from her cards. "Clo, she had some trouble with her knees." She threw a card on the table and grabbed another one.

"Was Ms. Thomas ever nervous about anything? Or maybe depressed?"

Nobody at the table answered. One of them traded in two cards. Finally, a couple of them shook their heads.

"She wasn't depressed about anything? Health? Finances? Loneliness?"

The angry man huffed. "What's this about?"

Earl motioned for Page to get out the digital camera. "If you could, please take look at a few pictures for us. Tell us if any of these people look familiar."

Page went to each person at the table, even the angry man, and showed each of them the set of digital photos. Throughout the process, Page asked whether any of them looked familiar.

Earl craned his neck, but he couldn't see the little picture screen from his chair. He had to be content with watching the faces of each person asked. He watched each set of eyes, waiting for any flickers of recognition.

There were none.

Once he was finished with the handheld slide show, Page put away his camera. He pulled out his notebook and pen to resume taking notes.

Earl looked at the old folks around the table. "So none of those faces were familiar to you?"

Everyone shook their heads. None of them took their eyes off their card game.

Earl bit his lip. For some reason, he had expected something different. He tried another tack. "Tell me, did Ms. Thomas go out much?"

The woman asked, "What, you mean on dates?"

The angry man demanded, "What do you get out of this?" He jabbed a finger in the direction of Page. "And why is he writing all this down?"

Earl focused on the woman. "Actually, I meant any reason at all. You know, maybe Ms. Thomas went to the movies, or maybe she went out to buy groceries. . . ."

"She pretty much liked to stay in. We have about everything we need here on the premises."

"Oh. Well, thank you for your time. If you can —"

"Of course, every Wednesday she went to the community center."

Earl scratched his nose.

Victor Caddigan's home was a shabby little house that needed a new lick of paint. The lawn was a lost cause. One second-story window was broken, marred by a baseball-shaped hole.

They went to the neighboring houses and knocked on several doors before they finally got an answer. A man came to the door in a fuzzy blue bathrobe and fuzzy pink slippers. "Yeah? What're ya selling?"

Earl forced himself to make eye contact. "Hello, sir. We want to ask a few questions about your neighbor."

"Oh! Don't get me started!"

"Sir?"

"People coming in and out all hours of the night, beer cans in the yard, they got cars parked up in my driveway here —"

"Um . . . I was referring to Victor Caddigan."

"Who? Oh. Don't know the lady. So, who's this poll for?"

Earl shifted in his wheelchair. "We came to the neighborhood to ask about the late

Mr. Caddigan." He nodded in the direction of the house, several doors over.

"Oh! Him!" The man scratched his belly. "That was a shame."

"Did you know him?"

"I saw him every so often. I mean, we didn't sit down for beers or nothin'."

"Of course." Earl nodded to encourage the man to continue.

The man nodded back. He didn't continue.

Page said, "Did he ever talk about his medication or anything?"

"Why would he talk about something like that? What business was it of mine?" The man squinted at them. "Who did you say you're polling for again?"

Earl tried to regain control of the conversation. "Actually, we were wondering whether Mr. Caddigan complained about his health. Maybe he was depressed or . . ."

"What are guys, doctors or something?"

Earl gave up and motioned for Page to get out his camera. "Sir, would you mind looking at a few pictures for us? We need to know whether you know any of these people. It could be really —"

"Listen, I got a pie in the oven." The door closed.

With a grimace, Earl put his hands to the

rims of his wheels and turned back down the driveway. Without a word, they went to the next house. And the next.

When they reached the end of the block, Earl decided to try the other side of the street. At the first house, a woman came to the door, a crying baby in her arms. She had no information for them.

Nobody at the next house. Or the next. At the house after that, the curtain in the picture window moved as someone peeked out. But no one came to the door.

Finally, at the house directly across from Caddigan's residence, a kid answered the door. His short red hair needed combing, and his freckled face needed a good wash. He was eating a cracker. He was probably about twelve years old.

Earl smiled. "Is your mom or dad at home?"

The kid, chewing, shook his head. He swallowed. "Pa's at the track."

"Oh." Earl motioned to Page they should move on. "Thank you."

"My ma's doing the laundry."

Earl stopped. "But you said —" He stopped himself and started over. "Young man, may we speak with your mother?"

The kid nodded and ran off. From somewhere inside the house, his voice echoed:

"Ma–a–a–a! Someone's at the door!"

Earl and Page waited on the porch. Finally, a tired-looking woman appeared at the door. She wore a blue jumpsuit, her hair tied up with a yellow cloth. She stopped chewing gum long enough to ask, "What're you fellas selling?"

Page said in a rush, "We're not selling anything; we need you to —"

Earl held up a hand. "Ma'am, we just want to ask a few questions about your neighbor, Mr. Victor Caddigan."

"Are you fellas with the newspapers or something?"

"No, ma'am, special investigators. Did you know Mr. Caddigan very well?"

"I'd visit him every few nights, sure. Whenever we had leftovers, I'd make him a plate and take it over."

"I see. Did he ever talk to you about his health or state of mind?"

The woman snapped her gum. "In what way?"

"You know, did he have any sort of illness, or was he depressed in any way . . . ?"

"What difference does that make?"

Page shot off, "If the Mercy Killer knew Caddigan was terminally ill or lost the will to live —"

Earl waved him to shush again. "Maybe

you could look at some pictures for us. Do any of these people look familiar to you?"

Page walked the lady through the various digital photos. Each time the response was negative. She had never seen Hamilton Page before, either.

Earl asked, "By any chance did Mr. Caddigan ever go to see one of Montague Black's stage shows? He was the celebrity psychic —"

"Vic didn't like to come outside. The neighbor kid would mow his lawn and take care of the flower beds for him. He'd only come out for church stuff."

"Oh. Just church, huh?"

"Yeah. Oh, and once a week his church's seniors group would take him out to some show at the community center."

Chapter Nineteen

Page dropped Earl at home so Earl could clean up and change for church. Earl hadn't heard from Gloria but assumed she'd pick him up for the meeting. He picked out his clothes, washed his face, rinsed and reinserted his dentures, the whole time mulling over what they'd learned the past two days.

No specific picture had formed yet, but Earl was feeling better about things than he had in days. There were a lot of little things, and he could see them begin to connect together. Years of driving the metro bus had given him a sharp eye as an observer, and that skill was going to come in handy here.

His thoughts were interrupted by an impatient bang at the door. The banging happened again, followed by a holler. "I know you're in there! Open up!"

Earl pulled on a shirt, wheeled cautiously to the door, and peeked through the curtain. It was Deputy Fisher — fuming. Earl fumbled with the dead bolt, opened the door, and looked up at the deputy.

The man's red face glared down from on high. "What have you been doing?" Earl had never seen him so furious. He started to ask the man inside, but the deputy pushed past him and started pacing the living room.

Earl swallowed. "To what do I owe the pleas—"

"I told you to butt out!" The deputy whirled and wagged his finger. "I told you people not to meddle! I told you people to mind your own business!" He began pacing again, hands to the sides of his head. "But you wouldn't listen! You had to obstruct a federal investigation!"

"Why don't you calm down before your head explodes?" Earl waved him toward the couch. "I find it hard to believe our little efforts have been any —"

"Until now, you've been beneath their notice. But now that you've expanded your operations, you're on their radar!"

Earl stiffened. "Really?"

"I should have arrested you when I had the chance! Do you know what will happen when they do figure out who you are? They are the *United — States — government.* Do you have any idea what they could do to you for interfering?"

Earl gulped. "What?"

Deputy Fisher shook his head. "If those FBI agents knew who's been out there asking questions . . ."

Earl started wringing his hands. "And they don't?"

The deputy collapsed onto the couch, burying his face in his hands. Finally, he looked up. His face had some of its normal coloring again. "I mean, your meddling into the murder of Black was a mild nuisance — you were trying to clear the name of your minister. But at least it was a case that was already done, wrapped up, and the sheriff was too busy with the FBI to even notice you. Why did you have to get involved in a federal investigation? Of a *serial killer?*

"This is still about the murder of Montague Black."

Deputy Fisher stopped dead, and his head tilted. "The Mercy Killer didn't murder Montague Black. These are totally unrelated."

"No." Earl sat back in the wheelchair, folding his hands in his lap. "They're connected."

The deputy regarded him suspiciously. "What evidence do you have?"

"Well, not *'evidence'* exactly, but I have a hunch if you —"

Fisher jumped up. "I knew it! You're addicted — this is like some drug for you!" He took a deep breath and let it out. When he spoke again, his voice was low. But the threat remained. "I should have hauled you in already. But I don't want to see you behind bars."

"I appreciate that."

"But you've got to end this obsession — right here, right now."

"But you didn't even —"

"Let me finish!" The deputy held up his hands. "Mr. Walker, did it ever occur to you that your life could be in danger? Or the life of your lady friend?"

Earl's eyes flashed. "Are you making some kind of threat?"

"Think about it. This Mercy Killer picks elderly folks as his victims. Now, can you think of any reason that would not also include you and Mrs. Logan?"

Earl opened his mouth. Nothing came out.

Towering over Earl, the deputy folded his arms. "See? You're not as smart as you thought you were." He took off his hat, held it in his hands a second, then put it back on his head. "If this comes up again, there will be an arrest. And if the FBI figures out who you are, it will be ugly." He adjusted his hat. "I'll see myself out."

After the deputy was gone, Earl sat thinking, clenching and unclenching his fists. He was so lost in his thoughts that he almost didn't hear the light tapping on the door. After a second, a familiar voice singsonged, "Hello!"

Earl opened the door for Gloria. She said, "I just passed the deputy in the parking lot. What'd I miss?"

The whole trip out to church, Earl kept to himself. A black cloud hung over him.

Behind the wheel, Gloria attempted to pry. "If you keep this bottled up, it's going to eat you alive. You sure you don't want to talk about it?"

"Not right now." Earl stared out the passenger window. Dusk was falling, and the streetlights began popping on, one by one. "I just need to think."

Reaching the parking lot of the church, they were shocked to see the large number of cars for a Friday night. Apparently, the main item on the agenda — whether to kick Pastor Benton to the curb, guilty or not — was a hot-button issue.

Generally, the church business meetings were in the basement. However, the meeting was moved to the sanctuary to accommodate the crowd. Judging from all the camera equipment and microphones, the media must have been out in force, too.

Fighting his way through the huddle in his wheelchair, Earl found his usual place in the sanctuary taken. Gloria found a space in one of the front pews. Earl parked his wheelchair in the aisle, where, unfortunately, passersby kept stumbling into him.

Somehow, Jenny found them. She expressed surprise that Earl would sit so close to the front. He could barely hear her over the buzz of the crowd. He shrugged and didn't try to answer.

Jenny squeezed into the pew next to Gloria and set her backpack down. As she dug through it for her Bible and a notebook, Earl noticed she had several folded newspapers. He motioned for her to pass them over.

A man walked up to the podium and tapped on the microphone, a *thump, thump, thump* echoing through the air. "If we can call this meeting to order . . ." The hubbub throughout the sanctuary reduced to a gurgling. "Bob, would you like to open us up with prayer?"

Out in the congregation, a man in one of the middle pews stood, bowed his head, and began to mumble. The room grew silent. Earl strained to listen, but he couldn't hear a word. Finally, the mumble stopped, and a wave of "Amens" washed through the sanctuary.

The man at the podium called up some old business and stepped back as a woman climbed the steps to the stage and took the microphone. She consulted her clipboard and began rattling off something or other.

Earl started leafing through the collection of newspapers, which went back the past couple or three weeks. He tried to find anything related to the recent string of murders — prior to and including Montague Black. He found a few stories of varying lengths here and there, but nothing really jumped out at him.

As the old business continued, Earl glanced around the congregation. The air crackled with a palpable nastiness to get to the topic everyone had come to argue. However, he didn't see the pastor or his family anywhere.

Turning back to his reading, he checked the obituary pages. Something nagged at the back of Earl's mind. Flickers of memory tormented him, images of the deputy yelling at him.

The man certainly had a point. It was one thing to risk the wrath of a small county sheriff, but the federal government? How far would they push a little old man in a wheelchair? Would they cut off his pension? Would they put him in prison?

The first man returned to the podium. "We'll discuss the Pastor Benton situation now. I guess the best way to handle this is to get right to the vote —"

A voice called out, "Aren't we going to discuss it first?" Another round of murmurs broke out.

The man at the front thumped the microphone again. "Order, order. Call to order. Now, Walt, I think everyone already knows what they feel about —"

"You're not going to convict the man without giving us a say, are you?"

The murmurs broke out again. The man thumped his microphone yet again. When the hubbub quieted, he said, "All right, if there are some folks who want their say, I suppose we can open the floor here." He instructed the man working the soundboard to get a wireless microphone out so they could pass it around. Hands shot up all over the big sanctuary — this would take awhile.

Earl settled back with his paper. He kept one ear open to the various testimonials. Roughly, it seemed to split evenly into two camps: those for standing by Pastor Benton and offering him moral support during this trying time, and those preparing to drag him down to the church basement and shove him in the furnace — do not pass go, do not collect two hundred dollars.

FOR: "Pastor Benton is always patient. How many times has he sacrificed his own time when a member of the congregation had a spiritual or physical need?"

AGAINST: "Did you see how awful he looked on TV? It doesn't matter whether he did it or not — the arrest is humiliating enough!"

FOR: "Pastor Benton is always willing to step in and help — like that time he directed the children's Christmas choir. Sure, it didn't turn out that great — but the man is deaf in one ear; give him a break!"

AGAINST: "What if Pastor Benton *is* the killer? Has anyone even thought of that?"

FOR: "Pastor Benton has an amazing work ethic. Whenever there's a project around the church, he's always willing to roll up his sleeves and get his hands dirty."

AGAINST: "Did you see those curtains in his office? The man is color-blind! In fact, I saw him with socks that didn't match his tie. I guess his wife was too busy to dress him that day. Bless her heart."

FOR: "Pastor Benton is always willing to

listen to your problems and share his advice. And when he can't help you, he always points you to someone who can."

AGAINST: "In the last election, the pastor refused to endorse God's candidate!"

FOR: "Pastor Benton is always full of the love of God and full of the Word of God and unafraid to express that ebullience and exuberance and . . ."

Earl tuned the man out.

AGAINST: "The pastor isn't keeping the parsonage lawn mowed properly. Have you seen what happened to it while he was in jail? It reflects poorly on the church."

That was the point where Earl got too aggravated to pay any more attention. He grabbed a short pencil out of the back of the pew in front of him. Each time he found an obituary that fit his criteria, he circled it. In the end, he had zeroed in on eight of them: Thomas, Snow, Zimmerman, Vollman, Buller, Fitzgerald, Anderson, Caddigan. All eight were seniors. Seven of them were listed as dying of "natural causes." This included those who would later be considered possible victims of the "Mercy Killer."

As he read the circled items, Earl focused on each detail. Where they were from. Where they lived. Who their families were. No common denominators leaped out at him. Of course, maybe the other five really did die of natural causes. People die all the time. But what if Montague Black had missed one or two?

Earl checked the dates. The correct order was actually Buller, Fitzgerald, and Anderson before the psychic got involved; Thomas, Vollman, and Caddigan were the three suspected victims of the so-called Mercy Killer; and then Snow and Zimmerman had both died after Black was out of the picture, the last one just the day before yesterday.

Most of them had lived in Fletcher County all their lives. One was originally from Scotland. One was born in Germany.

Five of the eight were survived by several family members — various combinations of brothers, sisters, cousins, sons, daughters, grandchildren, nieces, and nephews. A couple had just one or two survivors. One did not seem to have any known relatives.

Most of them left behind some kind of wealth. One was worth quite a lot of money. Two of them lost their —

Wait.

Earl flipped through the jumbled stack, searching for Thursday's paper. He found the obituary he needed. He read it once, twice. He turned to Gloria. "I figured it out."

Chapter Twenty

Eight o'clock Saturday morning, Earl was on the phone again with Deputy Landon Fisher. When Earl first asked his favor — admittedly, a big one — the deputy threatened Earl again with jail. But Earl convinced him of the value in reconstructing the crime — a French concept from one of Jenny's books.

Waiting for Gloria to pick him up, Earl forced himself to focus on the tasks at hand, moment by moment. Make the coffee. Take a shower. Shave. Pick out his clothes. Make breakfast. Put in his dentures. Eat breakfast. Get dressed. He ignored the doubts nibbling at the back of his mind. *Trust in the Lord,* he reminded himself, *trust in the Lord.*

Over his breakfast, his thoughts drifted back to the vote at church the night before. The numbers were close, but the congregation voted to stand by Pastor Benton, remembering a man's supposed to be considered innocent until proven guilty. Nonetheless, a committee was formed to field candidates for a possible replacement. Just in case.

When Gloria arrived, she was a bundle of nerves. "How can you not tell me what's going on? You've been keeping it to yourself for a week now."

"It's been twelve hours. Here, have some coffee."

Gloria poured herself a mug and sat at the kitchenette table. "This is driving me crazy. If you can prove how that man disappeared and framed the pastor, why don't you do something about it?"

"I *am* doing something. That's why we're going back out to that nursing home." He grunted. "I really am getting sick of that place."

"This is no time for grandstanding — the pastor is going to be tried for murder! If you figured something out, just tell the sheriff and be done with it!"

"Please — relax." Earl sipped his coffee, pretending he wasn't as nervous as she was. "If this goes like it should, the pastor will be cleared by lunchtime. And the naysayers at church will all feel very foolish."

They had some time before they had to leave, so they sat at the table, sipping their coffee. As Gloria stared into her mug, Earl watched her, thinking about the unfinished business between them. He felt his heart thumping in his chest again, wishing he could work up the nerve to tell her. . . .

He cleared his throat. "Hey, Gloria?"

She looked up uncertainly. "Yes, hon?"

"You know, we never did finish that conversation at the restaurant."

She smiled. "No. I guess we didn't."

He rubbed the back of his head, searching for the words. "Gloria, there comes a time —" There was a knock at the door. He grunted, "Excuse me."

It was Jenny at the door. Her timing was unwelcome, but Earl couldn't blame her — he'd invited her to come along for moral support.

Out in Gloria's car, the ladies pried more information out of Earl. He said, "You could say that Deputy Fisher and I had a heart-to-heart of sorts. We're going to reconstruct the crime. It's a French thing." Earl turned to Jenny in back. "I saw it in one of your books."

Jenny's eyes lit up. "Really? They helped?"

"As much as I hate to admit it."

Gloria glanced over nervously. "So, we're going to see all the suspects at the scene of the crime? Isn't that dangerous?"

"There's safety in numbers — if the guilty one tries something funny, the others will all be there. Besides, we'll have the deputy and the sheriff right there."

"If you say so," Gloria mumbled, gripping the steering wheel tightly. Her knuckles grew white.

"I'm more nervous about this not working out. What if I happen to be wrong?" Earl took a deep breath. "At least I'll only embarrass myself in front of five or six people."

When they reached Heritage Care, they found the parking lot packed — all the spaces taken, cars up in the grass, and vehicles along both sides of the road. Earl asked, "Are those media vans?"

Inside was a madhouse, shoulder-to-shoulder with people of all shapes, kinds, and sizes. Elbowing their way through the crowd were members of the media, wielding their implements of journalism like weapons.

Gloria asked, "What's going on?"

Earl grumbled, "I don't know. Why are all these people here?" Craning his neck, he finally saw Deputy Fisher across the crowded room. Hands on the rims of his wheels, he attempted to navigate his way through. "Excuse me!" Nobody noticed him. “Excuse me!”

Over in one corner they found the prayer group from the previous week, plus dozens more from church. The arguments from the night before were still going on. Pastor Benton and his wife were nearby but kept their distance.

Gloria waved. “Don’t worry, folks! Earl’s figured out the real killer!”

One woman strained to hear above the crowd. “The what?”

Gloria shouted, “The killer! Earl figured out the killer!”

Her words must have carried, because members of the media snapped to attention. Grabbing their microphones and cameras, they fought through the Wiccans and the Trekkies and the monks until they were close enough to shout at Gloria.

“Ma’am! What do you know about this operation?”

“Are you a special deputy?”

“Did you claim you can prove the reverend is the killer?”

As the lights and the cameras pushed in, Gloria turned white. “Um, you’ll have to talk to Earl.”

“Who is this ‘Earl’ guy you’re talking about?”

"Is that the name of the voice in your head?"

"Is this hypothetical 'Earl' in the room with us now?"

Earl growled, "I'm Earl! Now get out of my way!" Apparently, those nearest him finally noticed the man in the wheelchair and stepped out of his way. He pressed into the gap and shouted again, "Out of my way! Move it!" and so on, until he and Gloria and Jenny pushed through the throng to Deputy Fisher.

The deputy had to yell over the noise of the crowd. "About time you folks showed up! It took quite a few calls, but I got everyone here like you asked."

Earl raised his eyebrows. "I just said to make sure the suspects were here!"

"Right. Every person who was here last Saturday."

Earl felt his stomach drop. "There should only be five or six people here!"

"Oh. Well, you should've been more specific!" The crowd pressing around them, jostling him, the deputy tried to hold out his arms. "Because they're all here now!"

A voice bellowed over the noise, "What's going on here?" By the entrance, Sheriff Meyer was fighting the current, craning his neck, until his eyes locked on to Deputy

Fisher. In a rage, he surfed the wave until almost within arm's reach. "Would you care to explain what you think you're doing here?"

Deputy Fisher gulped. "Well, Sheriff . . ." He glanced at Earl then back at his superior. "Mr. Walker convinced me we should conduct an experiment. It's French."

The sheriff turned on Earl. "So you're the meddler who's been sniffin' around a federal investigation?"

"Well, I don't know that I would —"

"You listen to me, mister," the sheriff said, his voice rising in volume. "You leave police business to the professionals!" He turned to the younger man. "And Deputy, you are on report!"

Deputy Fisher nodded quickly. "Yes, sir."

Another voice roared over the crowd, "Meyer! Sheriff Meyer!"

Earl couldn't see the speaker for the crowd. However, the sheriff's white pallor indicated it was not good. Eventually they were joined by a pair of men in suits and dark glasses, earpieces wired to some hidden devices in their clothing.

The agents spoke to the sheriff, but Earl couldn't hear over the crowd. Finally, one of them turned his dark glasses on Earl. "So, this is the meddler? You'll be sorry when this gets into your file!"

Earl opened his mouth. Nothing came out. Earl tried not to squirm in his wheelchair. He had a file?

The agent turned to Sheriff Meyer. "I demand that you arrest this man!"

"Hold on! Hold on!" Somehow, Deputy Fisher pushed his way into the conversation. "We've spent the past week running around in circles, and we're not any closer than when we started. Now, if Mr. Walker can clear this up for us, don't you think it's worth hearing him out?"

The sheriff looked doubtfully from the deputy to the feds. The feds exchanged a glance and looked at the deputy.

"Besides," the deputy added, "the suspects are already here."

The sheriff and the feds exchanged another glance, then everyone stared down at Earl. The first FBI agent growled, "This better be good."

Earl nodded, never more scared in his life of going to prison.

The deputy got down on one knee next to Earl's wheelchair. "I don't have to tell you, Mr. Walker, that you better know what you're doing here."

"Uh-huh. I was just hoping for something a little more quiet."

The deputy couldn't hear over the noise. "What?"

Earl shouted, "I didn't want there to be so many people!"

The small group — Earl, the ladies, the deputy and the sheriff, and the FBI agents — left the crowded lobby for the relative quiet of the meeting room. As the deputy closed the door, Earl noticed his ears were ringing. He said, "Could we get all those people out of here?"

"You wanted to reconstruct the crime, didn't you? We need all these people here to do that!" The deputy put his hands on his hips. "Now, how do you want to play this?"

Gloria put a hand on his shoulder. "How are you going to explain how that man disappeared from this room?"

"Oh, that." Earl rubbed the back of his neck. "You know how when a magician tells you how he did his trick, it's such a letdown?"

Jenny nodded, quoting, "Everything becomes common-place by explanation."

One of the FBI agents said, "Sheriff, what are these people talking about?"

"I'm not sure. Deputy, what are these people talking about?"

"I'm not sure." Deputy Fisher knelt by Earl's wheelchair. "Mr. Walker, can we just get on with it?"

Earl rubbed his hands together slowly. "I guess we need to arrange the suspects."

The deputy frowned. "All of them?"

"Not the whole crowd," Earl growled. "I'm talking about Ms. Divina Zuniga, Mr. Hamilton Page, Ms. Sheree Jackson, and Mr. Jack Carpenter. We need to put everybody where they were when the murder happened."

"I see." The deputy stood. "It's kinda messy out there, so let's start by rounding everybody up into this room. It'll be easier to talk in here."

Deputy Fisher exited for the lobby. The feds pulled Sheriff Meyer to the other side of the room for a private conference.

Gloria and Jenny came close to Earl. While Jenny closed her eyes and prayed under her breath, Gloria knelt next to his wheelchair. "If you know what happened in here, why don't you just tell them?"

He rubbed his eyes. "There are a lot of little pieces that fit together. I just need everyone in one place at one time." He grunted. "Or maybe one of College's detective books has rubbed off and I'm an idiot."

Gloria squeezed his arm. "You're not an idiot."

He looked in her eyes. They were gorgeous. “Listen, maybe this isn’t the best time, but —”

The door swung open, and Jack Carpenter nearly leaped into the room. “Do you people have any idea how busy I am? I have appointments that I’m missing right now! I don’t have time for this!”

Following him into the room were Divina Zuniga, Ebenezer Wilson, Jack Carpenter, Hamilton Page, Sheree Jackson, and Pastor Andrew Benton. The deputy came in last, closing the door to shut out the noise of the crowd.

Ms. Zuniga let loose a combination of English and foreign words at the deputy, who held up his hands as if to fend off a physical attack. Ms. Jackson sulked in the corner, her arms folded around herself. Mr. Wilson stood silently, patiently. Pastor Benton leaned on the mantel of the fireplace.

Page saw Earl and stormed over. “Hey, we had a deal! If you found anything out, you promised to come to me first!”

The sheriff yelled, “Wait a second, these men are partners?”

Earl squirmed. “Not exactly.”

The sheriff threw up his hands. “I can’t believe this! This is clearly a conflict —”

The deputy held out a hand. “Now, you

promised to let Mr. Walker have his say, Sheriff. What can it hurt?"

The sheriff seethed. Finally, he turned back to his corner of the room with the feds. The federal agents said nothing; they just stood to the side, waiting for Earl to fail.

Deputy Fisher turned to Earl. "Now, Mr. Walker, you said that you wanted to put the suspects where they were at the time of the murder?"

Earl thought about the chaos outside the door. "Maybe we can just talk our way through it for the moment. That is, if we need to demonstrate —"

Ms. Zuniga huffed, "Let's get this over with. I have to get back to my editing."

Earl closed his eyes, reconstructing the scene in his head in the lobby from one week earlier. Then he looked up and pointed toward the door. "All right, ma'am, I remember you at the staircase, talking with some man. He was tall, and he was carrying something large on his shoulder."

"My cameraman, *si*."

He turned to Ms. Jackson. "And you were in the hallway, the one over on the left side of the lobby. You were eating candy. I believe you'd just been fired by your boss. Is that right?"

The woman blushed. "Yes."

Gloria whispered, "He's very observant."

Earl pointed at the gardener. "Mr. Wilson, you told us that you were outside in the garden. Why don't you go ahead and slide open that glass door?"

The man nodded and opened the door. He turned. "Do you want me to go outside?"

"You can stay with us for now. Thank you." Earl turned to Hamilton Page. "Okay, I remember that you were by the elevator."

"And you want me to go stand there now?"

Earl shook his head. "Not yet."

One of the FBI agents standing by shifted his weight from one foot to the other, letting out a big sigh.

Jack Carpenter sniped, "If this will get us out of here, I'll play along. At the time of the murder, I distinctly remember that I was making a statement to the press." He headed for the door.

Earl said, "Wait just a second, Mr. Carpenter."

The man turned, puzzled. "If you have any doubts, I'm sure one of these fellas outside has a video record of my statement to the press."

"Yes, you did make a statement to the press, but that was after the murder."

The man stopped. "No, I distinctly remember that when your reverend came in here . . ."

Pastor Benton raised a hand meekly. "He's right. I was the only one actually inside the room at the time of the murder."

The deputy said, "He's right, Mr. Walker. At the time of the murder —"

"Montague Black was already dead before that." Earl locked his fingers together. "The problem is that we all fell into the trap of thinking there were only two possibilities — either Pastor Benton here was telling the truth, or that he was telling a lie.

"For the sheriff, the choice was easy. The pastor had to be lying." Earl smiled. "As for those of us who believed in the pastor's innocence, however, we also believed his story. We were mesmerized by the possibility that some kind of trick happened in here — either the result of some illusion or, as Deputy Fisher here seemed to be hoping, demonic forces."

Everyone stared at Earl. He had them. "However, we were so busy taking sides, it never occurred to any of us that Pastor Benton was simply *mistaken.*"

Pastor Benton stood up straight. "What do you — ?"

Carpenter tapped his watch. "I'm sure we

all have places to be."

"Hold your horses — we're just getting to the good part." Earl turned to Ms. Jackson. "When were you out in the garden? In relation to the other things you were doing, I mean?"

She hesitated. "Um . . ."

"I'm sorry, I'm not being clear. Okay, you were outside looking for Mr. Black. When you came back inside, did you leave the sliding door open?"

She thought for a second and nodded her head. "Yes."

Carpenter, pacing in one corner of the room, whirled and yelled at the sheriff and the feds. "How much longer are we supposed to listen to this senile old man?" He marched purposely to the door, his dark mood forcing the others out of his way. "I think you've taken too much time already."

"Don't leave just as I'm getting to the good part, Mr. Carpenter — or should I say, Mr. Zimmerman?"

The man's hand froze on the knob. He looked at Earl, his eyes searching for a second. Then he chuckled. "I don't know what that was supposed to mean, but —"

Earl turned to the sheriff. " 'Carpenter' is the Anglicized form of the German family name 'Zimmerman.' With the recent death of Ingrid Zimmerman — a senior citizen who officially died of natural causes but is no doubt the true target of the Mercy Killer — I would imagine that Mr. Carpenter here is in line to inherit quite a bit of money."

Several mouths dropped open. One of the feds pulled out his cell phone and went to a quiet corner.

Carpenter narrowed his eyes. "That's crazy."

"Have you ever read a book by Agatha Christie called *The ABC Murders*? A friend of mine lent it to me." He glanced over at Jenny and winked. "It was very enlightening."

The sheriff blurted, "What in the Sam Hill does that have to do with the price of cows?"

"Carpenter needed to turn suspicion away from himself," Earl continued. "So he hatched an idea to kill several people so that Ingrid Zimmerman's death would be attributed to a fictitious serial killer." He turned and pointed at Carpenter. "You decided the best way to do this was to make use of your client, Montague Black. After all, he could drop convenient clues to the sheriff and pretend they were the results of psychic visions."

Carpenter started to open the door, but the deputy put a hand on the door and closed it. Page scrambled for his notepad and started scribbling.

Earl continued. "Black was doing the circuit of these old-folks homes and community centers and the like. So he was meeting all these senior citizens, learning about them. When you picked out your victims, your partner had already met them, had a chance to 'read' them."

"You're crazy. I never even met any of these —"

"We talked with several folks, and it seems pretty likely we can prove that Black met each of the victims before they were murdered and, by extension, that you had either also met or at least had access to his knowledge of them."

Carpenter sputtered, but no actual words came out.

"It must have been an ideal setup for you — it shaped the nature of the serial killer investigation and at the same time upgraded your client from a moderately successful stage hack into something of a celebrity. Soon your client was in demand by the national media — including a television contract with Ms. Zuniga, and the attention of a true-crime writer, Mr. Page."

Carpenter laughed, but it was hollow. He turned to the others and weakly pleaded,

"Can you believe this?"

Earl swiveled to speak to the sheriff. "But then Carpenter had a problem — the success of the hoax started to go to Black's head. He became unreliable. He was going to break his contract with Ms. Zuniga because he was offered a better deal. He refused to work with Hamilton Page because he thought he could get a better book deal himself."

He turned back to Carpenter. "And, of course, you had to worry about your own professional relationship with Black."

"Montague and I were best friends! He would have never —"

"But even worse for you," Earl continued, "Black knew that you were a murderer. And as he proved to be more unreliable, you began to wonder whether you could trust him. So, all this was already weighing on your mind when this public meeting was set up between Black and Pastor Benton."

Carpenter's mouth opened, but nothing came out. Earl glanced around and saw he had a captive audience. Even the agent was off the phone and listening.

"Now, when it was first brought to your attention, you were told that the church had set this meeting up. But after we were all here, you discovered that you had been lied to."

Carpenter licked his lips. "No, I wasn't."

Earl glanced at Ms. Jackson. "You set the whole thing up, didn't you? As a simple bid to trick your old lover into coming here? So you told Pastor Benton that Montague Black wanted to meet with him, and vice versa."

She nodded. She rasped, "Yes. I did that."

Earl turned back to Carpenter. "But you assumed the worst. You thought that it was Black who had set it up and lied to you about it. Then you had to wonder, why would he do that? You were already a nervous wreck; you were already waiting for him to betray you. Maybe you thought that he planned to make a confession to the minister, or make a public confession to the press."

Carpenter said, "That's crazy."

"When you tried to confront him, he blew you off. He didn't want to talk about it — and once again, you assumed the worst. You had no idea about the ill feelings between Black and Ms. Jackson here, no idea that he was agitated because he had also just found out that he was tricked.

"But you mistakenly thought his behavior confirmed your worst suspicions. Now certain that he was going to betray your secret, you panicked. In a fit of pure fear and blind rage, you grabbed a letter opener off that desk and stabbed him."

Carpenter huffed. "You can't be serious. There were a hundred people right outside that door!"

"Exactly! You were stuck. You were alone in the room with a dead man, and there were a hundred people standing outside. How could you possibly get away with it?

"So you hit upon the idea — it was such a slim chance, but it was all you had — you needed for someone to come in and find the body, see the open door, and assume the killer ran out through the garden."

"M–maybe that's what happened. Th–they could have —"

Earl looked at Mr. Wilson. "But there's no other way in or out of the garden, is there?"

Mr. Wilson stood upright. "No, sir!"

Earl turned to Carpenter. "So, not realizing there were two major flaws to your plan — one of which is the problem of the garden — you came out into the lobby and started working on your alibi. You schmoozed, you pretended to ask people the time, you made yourself as visible as possible."

The fed stepped toward Earl. "You said

there were two flaws. . . ."

Earl nodded. "Ah, yes. Mr. Carpenter here left Montague Black lying on the floor, but he didn't realize that Black wasn't actually dead yet." He turned to the rest of the room. "It's harder to kill a person in real life than it is in the movies. Back when I was driving the bus, there was this time —"

Gloria put a hand on Earl's arm. "Focus, dear."

"Ahem. Yes." Earl swiveled to the sheriff. "So Black comes to. He gets up, he pulls the letter opener out of his chest, he stumbles around. He's dying. He's disoriented. He probably meant to go outside, but as he collapsed against the glass panel there, he accidentally slid the exit closed. Finally, he stumbled behind the couch over there, where he collapsed."

Jenny asked, "But how did he disappear?"

Earl raised his eyebrows and held out his hands. "He didn't. After Black collapsed, he was back there the whole time." Earl locked his fingers together on his lap. "But for Mr. Carpenter's emergency alibi to work, he needed for someone to discover the body in here while he was out there. Of course, he'd expected the body to be sprawled in the middle of the room, the letter opener stuck in his chest, the glass door open to suggest that someone stabbed him and ran out the back way. He never expected the body to move itself."

He turned to Carpenter, who now leaned against the wall. "As the minutes passed and nobody found the body, you started to get worried. So you started sending people in here, hoping they would find the body and raise the alarm. That's the thing that struck me as odd at the time — you were so protective earlier, shielding your client, telling everyone, 'Don't talk to him, talk to me.' But suddenly, you went to those same people and told them, 'Go right on in, talk to him yourself.' "

Page looked up from his notebook. "Hey, that's right. I thought that was weird, too."

Earl folded his fingers into a steeple. "But Page didn't make it into the room. And Ms. Zuniga only got so far as looking in the door — where, unfortunately, she mistook Black's dying moments as meditation."

Ms. Zuniga gasped and covered her mouth with her hand.

Earl turned back to Carpenter. "As the minutes passed, it must have driven you crazy that nobody would cooperate by coming in here to find the body!"

Pastor Benton stood. "So when I came in here . . ."

Earl nodded. "The body was in here. But unlike the others, you sat down. And waited."

The pastor's face went white. "So, the moaning . . ."

"The man's dying gasp. He was on his stomach, so it was muffled by the carpet." Earl turned to the sheriff. "And with the acoustics in this room, and the fact that the pastor is hard of hearing in one ear, he thought the sound was coming out of the fireplace. So Pastor Benton goes over to check it out and steps on the letter opener. He picks up what is actually the murder weapon, thinking it's part of some prank, and storms out of the room."

Carpenter exploded. "Are you people actually listening to this old man? He's claiming that a man was dying in here, groaning, sliding doors, dropping a letter opener — and nobody heard it? There were a hundred people outside that door!"

Deputy Fisher asked, "Like now?" He opened the door, and instantly the room was filled with the noise of the crowd. "I bet we could shoot somebody right now and some of those folks would miss it."

Earl continued, "When the pastor came out and still hadn't noticed the body, Mr. Carpenter couldn't take it anymore —

someone *had* to find that body while he was out in the lobby making his alibi." He turned to Carpenter. "So you came to the door . . . but you were careful not to cross the threshold. You didn't want anyone to say that you were alone in the room with Black."

Carpenter took a breath. "You're crazy! I came to check on him. When I saw him lying there, I was too shocked to enter the room."

"That's just it — you stood in the doorway over there and proclaimed that Montague Black had been stabbed."

The sheriff scratched his head. "Well, he *was* stabbed. But the body wasn't behind the couch. It was way over here."

Earl smiled. "So Carpenter points and yells something like, "Grab that man! He killed Black!' And when everyone is looking the other way, Carpenter runs in, pretending to check on his friend, when he's actually dragging the body out from behind the couch. But he leaves the body facedown. A dead body is actually quite heavy."

Carpenter wheezed. "I was — I was trying to revive him. To, you know, check for vital signs."

"But if the body was all the way across the room and face down, how did you know that Black had been *stabbed?*"

Carpenter turned to the sheriff. "I didn't say that! He's putting words in my mouth!"

Earl turned his eyes to Ms. Zuniga. "With all those video cameras roaming the lobby at the time of the murder, how hard would it be to find out what Mr. Carpenter actually said?"

She narrowed her eyes at Carpenter. "Not hard at all."

Chapter Twenty-One

Saturday night, Gloria and Earl went out to dinner to celebrate. Following the debacle that was Maggiano's, Earl was not taking any chances. He asked around for recommendations.

He ended up with a short list that sounded decent. But in the end Earl went with the recommendation of Sheriff Meyer's, a place called Rockford's. The sheriff said that Rockford's was where he took his wife on their last anniversary. It was a nice place, they had steak, they had fish, and they had chicken. And the place was quiet — the point that mattered to Earl most.

Gloria dropped Earl off at his apartment and went home to change. Earl made a point to wash up, pick something nice to wear, and even took out his dentures and brushed them. He dropped them behind the sink but finally dug them out with the broom handle.

As he got himself ready, Earl kept thinking about what he might say to Gloria. It still made him wince to remember how badly it had gone the last time he tried to share his heart. He considered writing down a few words, but somehow creating a prepared speech didn't feel like the way to go.

As the time for Gloria's arrival neared, Earl wished that he'd had gotten some flowers for her. But he hadn't thought about it early enough to have called ahead of time and have them delivered. And if she was driving, he couldn't very well ask her to stop on the way. It just didn't seem right somehow.

Finally, at the appointed time, there was a knock at his door. When he opened the door, she grinned. "Why, hello there."

Earl struggled to find the power of speech. "Y–you're so lovely."

"Why, thank you! And you look mighty handsome."

There wasn't a lot of conversation in the car. The trip went much smoother than before; Earl had thought to call ahead. He had a reservation at six o'clock, and he had the driving directions written down.

The whole drive, Earl stared out the window, wondering what he might say to her. Wondering how it was going to work out.

They found the restaurant without incident. As they crossed the parking lot, Earl was nervous about any surprises. But after they got inside and saw the ambience — dim lighting, a candle on every table, and not one screaming kid insight — Earl's fears were put to rest.

At the table, they looked at their menus. They made small talk, although Earl was so nervous that he couldn't recall what they talked about. He kept looking into her eyes, he kept listening to her laugh, he kept thinking about her heart.

Finally, there seemed to be an opening. Gloria said, "I'm just glad it's all over now."

"I wouldn't say that it's completely over yet," he replied. "There's still some unfinished business."

"Really?" She looked puzzled. "What else can there be?"

Earl cleared his throat. This was it. "Gloria, there comes a time in a man's life when he . . . um . . ."

She reached across the table and put a hand on his arm. "What is it, hon?"

"I'm just having some trouble figuring out the words. Maybe if I could just —"

Suddenly, the waiter appeared. "What can

we get for you folks tonight?"

Earl gaped at the waiter. "Oh, I'm sorry, I didn't even look at my menu yet."

Gloria said, "Sure you did."

"Did I?" Earl flipped open the menu. "I can't remember any of it. Why don't you go ahead, and I'll figure it out."

Gloria ordered a steak sandwich and a baked potato. That sounded good enough to Earl, so he asked for the same. He was able to order some peppermint tea, and Gloria ordered some decaf coffee.

When the waiter left, Earl started over. "Let me just try again." He took a sip of his water, took a second sip, and wiped his mouth with the napkin. He cleared his throat. "Gloria, there comes a time in a man's life when he —"

A familiar voice interrupted him. "Hey, look who it is!"

Earl and Gloria turned to see Deputy Fisher and Jenny. Fisher was in plain clothes, and they were clearly on a date. Fisher said, "Long time no see, huh?" He guffawed.

"Wow," Earl said, trying — and failing — to keep the disappointment out of his voice. "What a surprise. Look, Gloria, it's Jenny and Deputy Fisher."

Gloria smiled. "Hello, dears. How are you

both doing?"

Jenny said, "We're doing well. Sorry to run into you like this. We just thought we'd grab something to eat before the show."

Fisher took one of the chairs. "Hey, what if we just sit with you guys?"

Earl exchanged a look with Gloria as Fisher pulled out a chair for Jenny. The deputy took the chair opposite for himself. "So, have you folks been settling okay?"

Earl looked at him. " 'Settling'?"

"You know, after all the excitement. I mean, that was quite a thing you did there today, man."

"Thank you. I think." Earl glanced at Gloria then back at the other man. "Considering what an ordeal the past week has been, we thought we would come out and celebrate."

Jenny asked, "So, have either of you heard about how Pastor Benton is doing?"

Gloria said, "Well, the Bentons are, of course, thrilled that he's been cleared. I think that several members of the church are going to be dropping by tonight to congratulate him, and in the process try to patch up some of their differences."

Earl shook his head. "I still can't see how some of those people could have voted against him like that. If the vote had gone their way . . ." He chuckled. "Even after the pastor was vindicated, that would be a hard thing to come back from."

"Well," Fisher said, "at least he's been cleared now. We all knew he was innocent."

Jenny made a face at him. "You're the one who locked him up!"

"Hey, I was just doing my job! Besides, I let you people solve the case." He locked eyes with Earl and blushed. He added, "Well, mostly."

Earl put a hand on Fisher's shoulder. "At least it turned out okay in the end."

The deputy held out his hand. "No hard feelings?"

Earl shook the hand. "No hard feelings."

"So tell me," the deputy said, "how did you ever connect Carpenter to Zimmerman?"

Gloria smiled. "Yeah, genius, how'd you do that?"

Earl sat back in the wheelchair, folding his arms. "There were a lot of little things — he collected beer steins . . . Montague Black's real name was 'Monty Schwartz,' which gave me the idea that Carpenter's family name could also have changed. 'Schwartz' is German for 'Black,' you know. The idea that there might be another murder after Black was unable to tell the police about it . . ."

Jenny stated, "I don't understand his plan at all. Why risk so much like that by killing all those strangers?"

Fisher said, "Makes sense to me. That is, the way Mr. Walker here explained it. Under normal circumstances, if this Zimmerman woman was murdered, the first person they would have looked at is the one person who stood to inherit her money."

Earl added, "By committing a lot of unrelated murders, he hoped to cloud the issue. Like in that book Jenny lent me." He winked at her. "Good job, College."

She blushed. "Thank you."

Fisher grinned. "After we got Carpenter back to the station, he broke down and told us the whole thing. He had gambling debts, and he owed some men a lot of money. When he found out about this distant cousin of his — and that she had a fortune locked away — he decided to kill her for the money."

Gloria whispered, "That's crazy."

Earl shrugged. "Crazy people do crazy things."

Jenny frowned. "I'm just glad all those video cameras were there! I mean, what if it had come down to your word against his?"

Fisher looked around. "I wonder where

that waiter is?"

Earl leaned over and whispered to Jenny, "Look, College, I don't want to seem like I'm not glad to see you kids — but scram!"

Jenny looked from Earl to Gloria then back to Earl. Her eyes widened, and she clutched Fisher's arm. "Hey, Landon, we should really leave them to their dinner. Let's get our own table."

He looked at her. "You think so? I wouldn't want to be rude. . . ."

"We really, really should."

The four politely said their good-byes. The kids went to ask the hostess for their own table.

Earl was relieved to be alone with Gloria, but it was short-lived. The butterflies in his stomach reminded him that he still didn't know what to say. All he could think of was "Good kids."

"Yes, they are." Gloria looked in his eyes, and her lips spread into a grin. "So, I do believe that you were saying something before."

"Yes, I was, wasn't I?" He grabbed the water off the table and gulped. He set it down, thinking a silent prayer. He cleared his throat. "Gloria, there comes a time in every man's life when . . . when . . ." He drew a blank.

She looked at him. Her eyes sparkled. "Yes?"

He sighed. "I'm sorry. I guess I just don't know how to say this."

Her eyes narrowed with concern. "Don't know how to say what, hon?"

"I've been alone for a long time, since the death of my Barbara. In all these years since she passed away, it never occurred to me that I could love again. It just didn't seem possible."

Gloria squeezed his hand, and he got flustered.

Earl found his voice and continued, "But then we . . . that is, you were . . . I mean . . ." He sighed. "I haven't proposed to a woman in fifty years. So I guess I'm a little out of practice."

Gloria leaped out of her chair and seized him. "I think you asked just fine!"

"I did?"

"Yes!"

He hugged her back. "Really?"

"Absolutely, you big, frustrating man!"

As she took her chair again, Earl grinned so big he almost lost his dentures. He whirled around to see where Jenny and Fisher were sitting and got Jenny's attention. "Hey! College!" He gave her a thumbs-up. She must have read the grin and the thumb correctly, because she returned them.

Through the rest of dinner, Earl and Gloria discussed their future together. Earl could barely eat — he was elated, he was scared, he was invigorated. After years as a bitter, lonely old hermit, he was opening up his life to someone else. His life was about to change forever. And he couldn't be more thrilled.

After all, what was the worst that could happen?

ABOUT THE AUTHOR

Chris Well has spent most of his adult life writing for and editing magazines, including Bill and Gloria Gaither's *Homecoming Magazine, Christian Bride,* and *Alfred Hitchcock's Mystery Magazine.* Also a novelist and a longtime fan of detective stories, Chris is thrilled to be writing his first series of cozy mysteries. He and his wife make their home in Tennessee, where he is hard at work on his next novel(s). Visit him online at www.StudioWell.com.

You may correspond with this author by writing:
Chris Well
Author Relations
PO Box 721
Uhrichsville, OH 44683

The employees of Thorndike Press hope you have enjoyed this Large Print book. All our Thorndike, Wheeler, and Kennebec Large Print titles are designed for easy reading, and all our books are made to last. Other Thorndike Press Large Print books are available at your library, through selected bookstores, or directly from us.